Sarah Crossan

Sarah Crossan has lived in Dublin, London and New York, and now lives in Hertfordshire. She graduated with a degree in philosophy and literature before training as an English and drama teacher at Cambridge University. Since completing a masters in creative writing, she has been working to promote creative writing in schools.

To find out more about Sarah and her sensational books visit **sarahcrossan.com** and **@SarahCrossan**.

the WEIGHT of WATER

APPLE
AND
RAIN

'This poignant, realistic tale is about learning to love and
taking responsibility, and about how poems can tell the
truth, as Emily Dickinson put it, at a "slant"'
Sunday Times

'Crossan's skill as a writer is at its most pronounced,
contributing to a portrayal of adolescence that is
subtle and humane'
Irish Times

'An inspiring tale'
Irish Examiner

'It'll make you laugh and cry ...'
Company

One

Sarah Crossan

BLOOMSBURY

LONDON OXFORD NEW DELHI NEW YORK SYDNEY

Bloomsbury Publishing, London, Oxford, New York, New Delhi and Sydney

First published in Great Britain in August 2015 by Bloomsbury Publishing Plc
50 Bedford Square, London WC1B 3DP

www.bloomsbury.com

Bloomsbury is a registered trademark of Bloomsbury Publishing Plc

A CIP catalogue record for this book is available from the British Library

Hardback ISBN 978 1 4088 6311 4
Export ISBN 978 1 4088 7234 5

MIX
Paper from
responsible sources
FSC
www.fsc.org FSC® C020471

Typeset by RefineCatch Limited, Bungay, Suffolk
Printed and bound in Great Britain by CPI Group (UK) Ltd, Croydon CR0 4YY

1 3 5 7 9 10 8 6 4 2

For Ben Fox (1988-2014)
— ride on

AUGUST

Here
    We Are.

And we are living.

Isn't that amazing?

How we manage
to be
at all.

The End of Summer

Summer's breath begins to cool.
The ink of night comes earlier and earlier.
And out of the blue
Mom announces that Tippi and I
will no longer be taught at home.
'In September
you'll join a class of juniors
and go to school
like everyone else,' she says.

I don't make any
                     ripples.

I listen
and nod
and pull at a loose thread in my shirt
until a button

falls away.

But Tippi doesn't stay silent.

She detonates:

Are you *kidding* me?
Have you lost your *minds*?' she shouts,
then argues with Mom and Dad for hours.

I listen
and nod
and bite at the skin around my fingernails
until they start to

bleed.

Finally Mom rubs her temples, sighs, and gives it to
   us straight.
'Donations from well-wishers have dried up
and we simply can't afford to homeschool you.
You know your dad hasn't found a job yet
and Grammie's pension
doesn't even cover the cable bill.'

'You girls aren't cheap,' Dad adds,
as though all the money spent on us
        —the hospital bills and special clothes—
could be saved if we'd both
only
behave a little better.

You see,
Tippi and I are not what you'd call normal—
not what you see every day
or *any* day
for that matter.

Anyone with a jot of good manners
calls us 'conjoined',
though we've been dubbed other things, too:
freaks, fiends,
monsters, mutants,
and even a two-headed demon once,
which made me cry so hard
I had puffy eyes for a week.

But there's no denying our difference.

We are literally joined
        at the hip—
                united in blood and bone.

And
        this
is why
we never went to school.

For years we've been cooking up chemistry potions
on the kitchen table
and using our yard for P.E.

But now
there's no getting out of it;
we *are* going to school.

Not that we'll be in a state school
like our sister Dragon,
with kids who pull knives on teachers
and drink Tipp-Ex for breakfast.

No, no, no.

The city won't fund our homeschooling but
they'll pay
for a place
at a private school
—Hornbeacon High—
and Hornbeacon is willing to have that one place
count for the two of us.

I guess we're supposed to feel lucky.

But lucky isn't really how
I would
ever
describe us.

Everyone

Dragon stretches out on the end of the double bed
I share with Tippi,
her bruised feet pointed while she
paints her toenails a deep metallic blue.
'I don't know,
you might like it,' she tells us.
'Not *everyone* in the world is an asshole.'
Tippi takes the polish, starts on my right hand and
blows my fingernails
dry.
'No, you're right,
not everyone's an asshole,'
Tippi says.
'But around *us*,
        they all morph into them.'

A Freak Like Us

Dragon's real name is Nicola,
but Tippi and I changed it
when she was two,
when she was fierce and fire-breathing,
stomping around the apartment and
chomping on crayons and toy trains.

Now she's fourteen and a ballet dancer
she doesn't stomp anywhere—
she floats.

Lucky for her she's completely normal.

Although

I do wonder if being our sister
        sucks sometimes,

if being our sister
makes her a freak
too.

Ischiopagus Tripus

Although scientists have come up with ways to
categorise conjoined twins,
each and every pair that ever existed
is unique—
the details of all our bodies remain a secret
unless we want to tell.

And people *always* want to know.

They want to know exactly what we share
        down there,
so sometimes we tell them.

Not because it's their business
but to stop them wondering—it's all the
  wondering
about our bodies that bothers us.

So:
Tippi and I are of the ischiopagus tripus
  variety.
We have
two heads,
two hearts,

two sets of lungs and kidneys.
We have four arms as well,
and a pair of fully functioning legs
now that the vestigial leg has been
                              docked
                              like a show dog's tail.

Our intestines begin
        apart
        then merge.

And below that we are
        one.

It probably sounds like a prison sentence,
but we have it better than others
who live with fused heads or hearts,
or only two arms between them.

It really isn't so bad.

It's how it's always been.

It's all we know.

And actually,
	we're usually
	quite happy
	together.

Milk Trudge

'We're out of milk,' Grammie says,
brandishing an empty milk carton and
a mug of steaming coffee.

'Well, go and get some,' Tippi says.

Grammie wrinkles her nose and pokes Tippi's side.
'You know I have a problem with my hip,' she says,
and I laugh out loud;
Grammie is the
only person on the planet who ever pulls
The Disability Card
with us.

So Tippi and I trudge to the corner store
two blocks away,
which is how we get everywhere:
trudging
        and lumbering
                along,
my left arm around Tippi's waist,
        my right slung over a crutch—
                Tippi mirroring me.

By the time we reach the store we are both
breathing hard
and neither of us wants to carry the milk home.
'She can run her own errands in future,' Tippi says,
stopping
for
a moment and
leaning on some rusty iron railings.

A woman pushing a stroller passes by,
her mouth
a gaping cavern.
Tippi smiles and says, 'Hey there!'
then snickers
when this woman with a perfectly formed body
almost topples over in surprise.

Picasso

Dragon spreads a thousand jigsaw pieces
                    across
the kitchen table.

The picture on the box promises that the mess will
turn into a
painting by Picasso
        —'Friendship'—
a surreal arrangement of
        limbs
and lines,
        of solid blocks of
        yellow,
        brown, and
        blue.

'I like Picasso,' I say.
'He paints the essence of things
and not only what the eye can see.'

Tippi huffs. 'It looks impossible.'

Dragon turns the pieces
        face up.

'The harder the better,' she tells us.
'Otherwise, what's the point?'

Tippi and I plop ourselves next to her
on an
      extra-wide dining chair
as
Dad
   shuffles
     down
     from his bedroom
bleary-eyed and smelling stale.

He watches us
rummaging to find the puzzle's frame
     —the edges
     and corners—
then reaches over Dragon's shoulder
and places in her palm
the top right-hand corner piece.

He sits at the table opposite us
and silently slides bits we've been looking for
into line.

'Great teamwork,' I say,
beaming at Dad.

He looks at me and winks.
'I learned from the best,' he says,
and gets up from the table to search in the
  refrigerator for a
beer.

The Launch

Mom and Dad prepare Tippi and me
for our first day at school
like they are
      launching astronauts
                into space.

Every day is packed with appointments.

They arrange for us to see our
therapists, doctors, and dentist.
Then Grammie highlights our hair
and shapes our nails
so we will be ready for our
      Great Public Appearance.

'It's going to be *fabulous*!' Mom says,
pretending we aren't being
thrown into a ring of lions
without a weapon,
and Dad smiles
      crookedly.

Dragon, who's about to become a freshman,
rolls her eyes

and tugs at the cuff of her cardigan.
'Oh, come on, Mom,
don't pretend like it's going to be easy.'

'Well, I'm leaving if I hate it,' Tippi announces,

and Dragon says,
'I hate school. Can *I* stay at home?'

Grammie is watching *Judge Judy*.
'Why would anyone hate school?' she caws.
'Best days of your lives, girls.
You'll meet your sweethearts there.'

Dad turns away,
Dragon blushes,
and Mom doesn't speak
because
they all know
that finding love is
something
that will never
        happen
        for us.

Therapy

'Tell me what's going on,'
Dr Murphy says,
and as
so often happens
I sit in silence
for ten whole minutes,
worrying at a button in the brown leather sofa.

I've known Dr Murphy
all my life, sixteen and a half years,
which is a long time to know anyone
and to have to think of new things to say.
But the doctors insist we come for regular therapy
to support our mental health,
as though that's the bit of us that's broken.

Tippi is wearing headphones and listening to loud
  music
so she can't hear what I'm saying,
so I can
spew all my suppressed feelings into
Dr Murphy's notebook
without hurting any of Tippi's.

And I used to rant a lot,
when I was seven or eight,
and Tippi had stolen my doll
or pulled my hair
or eaten my half of a cookie.

But now there's not much to say
Tippi doesn't already know,
and the talking seems
a waste of money we don't have
and of fifty perfectly good minutes.

I yawn.

'So?'
Dr Murphy says,
her forehead furrowed
as though my problems are her own.
Empathy, of course,
is all part of the service.

I shrug.

'We're starting school soon,' I say.

'Yes, I heard.
And how do you feel about that?' she asks.

'Not sure.'
I look up at the light shade,
at an unspoiled web and a spider gorging
on a fly bigger than itself.

I fold my hands in our lap.
'Well . . .' I say,
'I suppose I'm afraid the other students will pity
   me.'

Dr Murphy nods.
She doesn't tell me
they won't
or
that it's going to be fantastic
because lies are not her style.
Instead she says, 'I'll be really interested
to hear how it goes, Grace,'
and looking at the wall clock
chirps,
         'See you next time!'

Tippi Talks

We go next door
into Dr Netherhall's office
where it is my turn to wear the headphones
and Tippi's turn to tell all.

Which
I think
she actually does.

She talks quickly,
her expression serious,
her voice
sometimes loud enough for me to catch
     a stray
word
or two.
I turn the music up,
force it to swallow the sound of her
and then I watch
as
she
crosses her foot over mine,
uncrosses it,
pushes her hair out of her face,

24

coughs,
bites her lips,
wriggles in our seat,
scratches her forearm,
rubs her nose,
stares at the ceiling,
stares at the door,
all the time
talking
until
finally she taps my knee
and mouths the word
'Done.'

The Check-up

Mom drives us all the way to the specialist
  children's hospital
in Rhode Island
for our quarterly check-up,
to ensure our organs aren't making plans to
  pack it in.
And today,
like every other time before,
Dr Derrick parades his
        wide-eyed
medical students
and asks if we mind them
watching the exam.

We mind.

Of course we mind.

But Dr Derrick's stethoscope and white coat
do not permit disagreement
so we shrug
and allow ourselves to be
ogled
by a dozen trainee doctors
with tight mouths

and narrow eyes
who
        tilt forward,
        ever so slightly
        on their toes,
as we lift our shirts.
By the end we are blushing
and only want to
                    leave.

'They're all good?' Mom asks hopefully
when we're back in Dr Derrick's office.
He taps the top of his
desk.
'Everything clear
as far as I can see,'
he says.
'But as always,
they have to take it easy,
especially now they'll
be at school.
Right?'
He points a playful warning finger at us.
'Right,' we say,
not planning to
change a thing
about how we live.

Influenza

Two days after our visit to
Dr Derrick
it knocks us down
flat on to our backs
        without any warning.

I shiver and shake
        and cling to the duvet
        popping two white tabs of paracetamol
into my mouth every four hours,
hoping
to keep the chills away.

Tippi is lying next to me
shuddering,
sneezing, coughing,
and making her way through
a second box of Kleenex.

Our sheets are wet with sweat.

Mom delivers boiling
drinks
and tries to make us
eat a little toast.

But we are too sick
to move.

I Cannot Shake It Off

I cannot get these shivers to go away
and though Tippi seems way better
she has to stay in bed, too.

While I
      fight the flu.

Worrying

Mom calls Dr Derrick
and gives him
    a list
    of our
    symptoms.

He isn't worried,
for now.
He tells her to keep us hydrated
and in bed for a few more days.

He tells her to watch us.

But Mom can't help watching.

She can't help worrying.
    And why wouldn't she
    when so few of us manage to make it to
    adulthood.

The older we get
    the more she frets.

As time ticks by
the chances of us
             suddenly
ceasing
to be
get
quite
high.

That's just a fact
that will
never
go
away.

I Get Up

I don't want to.
My legs are wobbly.
My throat is coated in sand.
And my heart feels as though it's beating
extra hard
just to
get me from the bed
to the bathroom.
'You sure you don't want to lie down?'
Tippi asks.
I shake my head.
I can't confine her to bed
just because I can't get my
act together.
I shake my head

and suck it up.

SEPTEMBER

Almost

The front door opens and closes
and Dad's voice calls out,
'Hello? Anyone home?'

We are so close to finishing the jigsaw puzzle
we don't shout back.
We don't even look up.
All we want is to conquer this Picasso,
these masses of colour.

'I got you presents!' Dad says,
sweeping into the kitchen and
throwing two bags right
on top
of the puzzle.

We hold our breaths.

Dad rummages.

He pulls out two boxes and
hands them to
Tippi and me.

I gasp.

Phones—
brand new,
still wrapped in cellophane.

'Oh my God,' I say.
'Are you serious?'

Dad smiles.
'You'll need them for school tomorrow.
They're state-of-the-art
and they're new.
For my girls.'

'I thought we had no money,'
Tippi says.

Dad ignores her and hands a larger box
to Dragon.
'And for you,' he says.

Dragon peers inside,
        blinks,
and takes out a pink satin
ballet slipper.

She turns it over to look at the sole.

'They're nice,' she says.

'But they're too small.'

The fan in the corner of the kitchen whirs.
Dad stares at her steadily.

'They're too small
is all,' Dragon tells him.

Dad sighs.
'I just can't win, can I?' he says.

He grabs the shoebox from Dragon,
pitches it back into the bag,
and pulls the lot
down from the table,
taking every last piece of Picasso
with it.

Truth Is What Happens

Tippi,
half dipped in sleep,
drains her coffee mug and
stares into her scrambled eggs
as though she can read her future in the
yellow and white
      swirls.

I never
usually
rush her,
but we can't be late,
not on our first day of school,
so I quietly clear my throat
      —*ahem, ahem*—
hoping it will stir her from daydreaming long
  enough
to get going on the marbled eggs.

Instead it is like pouring
icy water into a
pan of hot fat.

Tippi pushes away her plate.
'You know I'm owed a
goddamn gold medal
for all the times you've kept *me* waiting
over the years.'

So I whisper,
'I'm sorry, Tippi,'
because I can't lie and pretend the
throat clearing
meant nothing.

Not with her.

Truth:
It's what happens
when you're bound like we are
by a body too stubborn
to peel itself apart at conception.

Uniform

Unlike Dragon's school
where they can wear what they like,
Hornbeacon expects all students to wear
uniforms—
bright white shirts, stripy green ties,
a plaid skirt
        with pleats down the front.

The idea
is to make everyone look the same.
I know that.
But it doesn't matter how we dress.
We will always
                stand out,
and trying to look like everyone else is stupid.

'It isn't too late to back out,' Tippi says.

'But we agreed to go,' I reply,
and Tippi clicks her tongue.

'I was forced into saying yes.
You think I want *this*?' she asks.
She tugs at the tie knotted around her neck,

pulling it up
and into a noose.

I reach for the skirt and step in.
Tippi doesn't resist
but pulls it into place.

'I feel so ugly,' Tippi says.

She laces her fingers through my hair and
        separates it into three thick strands
        which she plaits and unplaits.

'You're not ugly.
You look like me,' I say, smirking,
and squeeze her hand
tight.

What Is Ugly?

I've been in enough hospital wards to have seen
  horrors:
a kid with his face melted down one side,
a woman with her nose ripped off and ears hanging
loose
        like strips of bacon.

That's what people call ugly.

Not that I would.

I've learned to be less cruel than that.

But I know what Tippi means.

People find us grotesque,
especially from a distance,
when they see us as a whole,
the way our bodies are distinctly two
        then merge,
        suddenly,
        at the waist.

44

But if you took a photograph of us, head and
  shoulders only,
then showed it to everyone you met,
the only thing people would notice is that we are
  twins,
        my hair to the shoulders,
Tippi's a little shorter,
both of us with pixie noses
and perfectly peaked eyebrows.

It's true to say we're different.

But ugly?

Come on.

Give us a break.

Dragon's Advice

If I'm being completely honest,
school's probably the worst place you'll ever go in your life.
Seriously.
Middle school is bad
but I hear high school is hell.
The kids are mean and the teachers are bitter.
Really.
Listen,
whatever you do, don't get stuck with the first kids who
want to hang out
with you
because chances are no one else likes them.
That's social death.
And in the cafeteria, sit as far away as you can from the
  jocks.
I mean it.
And I know this sounds weird, but if you need to poop,
wait until you get home.
Bathrooms are for cigarettes and make-up.
That's it.
OK?
I'm sure you'll
be fine.

Mom

'Time to go,' Mom says.
She jangles the car keys and
    steps into the hall.

Her hair is wet.
Damp spots bloom on the
    shoulders of her shirt.

Mom does not dry her hair any more,
nor straighten it.
The only indulgence she allows herself
is a smear of gloss on her lips
    sometimes.

She never used to look so plain.

She used to have time to do herself up,
but that was before Dad's college
made cutbacks and let him go,
before Mom took on extra hours at the bank.

I can't remember the last time I saw her
flick through a magazine
or sit to watch something on TV.

I can't remember Mom being still for more
than a moment.

Her life now is
work,
work,
work.

So despite my sweating hands and the sick feeling
  in my stomach,
and regardless of whether or not
Tippi and I want to go to school,
we will go.

We will go,
and we will
not complain.

Hornbeacon High

The building is white,
ivy eating its way up the broken walls,
windows small
and scratched.

Most students are
pulling at one another and squealing,
basking in their easy, friendly reunions.

But I
study those
who are alone,
at the edge of this noise,
the kids holding their school bags close,
keeping their eyes down,

so I can
impersonate their
invisibility.

Among Wolves

'You will not be thrown to the wolves,'
Mrs James, the principal, says,
and presents Yasmeen—
a student to be our guide,
'and friend . . .

      for a while,' Mrs James says.

Mom and Dad look relieved,
as though this girl with a conspicuous hot pink
  bob and
skinny wrists
could fend off more than a moth.

'Holy cow!
You guys are *amazing*!' Yasmeen says,
without looking sickened,
which is, I think,
a pretty good start to the day.

And what she's said
      is true.

It *is* amazing we survived
      the womb.

Amazing we didn't die
        at birth.
Amazing we've lived as long as
        sixteen years.

But I don't want to be amazing.
Not here.

I want to be as boring as everyone else
though I don't tell Yasmeen this.
I smile and Tippi says, 'Thanks,'
and we follow our tiny
pink-haired defender along the hallway
to class.

Eyes

Tippi can't stand clowns.
Dragon is terrified of cockroaches
and Mom of mice.
Dad pretends to be fearless,
though I've seen him flinch when the mail arrives,
seen him hide
        hospital bills and parking tickets under
        stacks of junk mail and old newspapers
in the hall.

Me?
It's eyes I despise.
Eyes,
        eyes,
                eyes
                        everywhere,
and the probability that I'm
another person's nightmare.

So when Yasmeen opens the door to our homeroom
and every head
turns
        slowly,

I grab Tippi's right wrist
like I always do when
I'm afraid.

'Welcome! Welcome to Hornbeacon!' the teacher
  says,
doing everything she can to sound natural.

Yasmeen groans, leads us to some seats at the back.
And the whole way there we are
followed by a field of open mouths,
thirty pairs of bugging-out eyes,
and one hundred percent pure
panic.

In Homeroom

Mrs Jones
reads through the school rules,
allocates lockers,
and hands out personalised schedules.
Yasmeen grabs ours
before Tippi and I have
a chance to look at it.
She runs a finger
down
the
columns,
          along the rows.
'We're together for most subjects.
Awesome,' she says,
and claps me hard
on the back
like she's known
me for
years.

Maybe More Than That

For all her silly hair
and thin bones
Yasmeen is not delicate or lace-winged.

She swears at anyone who gives us
a slanted look
and threatens
to break the fingers of a freshman
who smirks when he sees us.

Yasmeen doesn't have an entourage
like the prettiest girls,
the blonde ones with bouncing breasts and
invisible bottoms,
but still,
no one gets in her way.

And she seems to have only one friend,
or maybe he's more than that,
a boy called Jon
who introduces himself in art,
holding out his hand and

looking at Tippi and me
in turn
like we truly are
two people.

Art Class

'God I hate being back,' Jon says,
yawning and battering a clot of grey clay
with a rolling pin until it is
     flat.
His eyes are walnut brown and quiet.
His hair is shaved so tightly to his head
he could be in the army.
His hands are speckled in tiny tattoos—
stars that seem to twinkle as he moves
his fingers
through the clay.

'At least you get to see me every day,'
Yasmeen says huskily
and nips and tucks at her own clay piece
     until it is a lopsided pot.

'I'm Tippi. This is Grace,' Tippi tells Jon,
talking for both of us.

But
I want to speak
     for myself.

I want Jon to hear my voice,
though I sound identical to my sister.

And I want his eyes focused on me
as they are focused on Tippi:
still
and without the tiniest
hint of horror.

In Our Free Period

In the common room
they crowd around
like we are
lunch
and they are
       starved animals ready to feed.

Necks long
       —stretched and taut—
              they strain to see.

It isn't as though we're performing
a butt-naked cancan routine.
All we are doing is
leaning on our crutches.

Yet this is enough.

Our very beings keep them mesmerised.

The spectators are girls with
smooth hair,
boys with collars
       turned up,

their nails clipped and clean,
and as a pack they look like a scene
from an Abercrombie & Fitch catalogue—
everyone groomed and carefully ironed.

No one speaks
when
Tippi tells them our names
and where we're from.
They just look at us
steadily
as though checking
we are real.

Yasmeen eventually drives off the crowd.
'Enough!' she shouts
and leads us to plastic seats by a fire exit.

Jon says, 'I guess the staring
stops bothering you after a while.'

'Would it stop bothering *you*?' Tippi asks.
I swallow.

Yasmeen snorts.

Jon thinks about this for a moment.

'No,' he says.

'It would piss me
the hell off.'

French

I do not listen to Madame Bayard explaining how
our grades will be calculated over the semester.
I ignore her ice-breaking explanation
for how to make one's own *chocolatine*.
And I don't even bother copying down the
  homework
because
Jon is to my right
where Tippi is
not,
and he is hurling questions at me
like I'm on a late night talk show,
sitting in one of those square chairs,
and not on trial,
which is how most people make me feel
when they get inquisitive.

'Do you both have passports?' he asks.
        'Yes,' I tell him.
        'Not that we use them.'

'And you never want to punch your sister's lights
out?'
        'Not usually.'

'So why come to school now?
Why here?'
    'No choice.'

'Oh, yeah. I get that, Grace.
Totally.'

He gnaws at the end of his pencil,
thrums his fingertips
against the desk.

'No choice . . .
I get that.
If I wasn't here
I'd be on a very slow train
to nowhere.'

The Cafeteria

As we enter the cafeteria,
Yasmeen and Jon
dance around us,
      one in front
one behind
so we are not
      quite
      seen.

Mom, Dad, Dragon, and Grammie
have been this doing for years,
hiding
us
as best they can
from ridicule
and camera phones,
because there's nothing worse
than a *click-click-click*
and knowing that in seconds
you'll be famous via
someone else's social feed.

We order chipboard pizza,
a Sprite with two straws,

and sit
     at a corner table
     with Yasmeen and Jon,
talking over
other voices and clinking cutlery,
not about how we live
     —the logistics of conjoined pissing—
(which is how I thought the whole day would be)
but about movies
and music
and books
and beer
and the new school year
and the islands of Greece
and coral reefs
and our favourite cereals
and Satan.

We have perfectly silly conversations
and by the time the bell rings
I am starting to wonder—
have we
found ourselves
     two friends?

Where?

We have cousins
who tolerate us
and a sister we hang out with sometimes.

But friends?

Where would we have found those?

Touch

Tippi and I are standing at the lockers
switching out our books
when a heavy-set girl from our homeroom
stops by us,
her eyes on the floor.

'Are we in your way?' Tippi asks.

The girl pales.
'No. My locker's next to yours.
But take your time,' she whispers.

'There's plenty of room,' Tippi says,
shifting her weight my way.

The girl shakes her head,
steps back a couple of inches.

Oh.

She's scared to come any closer.
She's scared that if she puts her hand
into her locker for a textbook,
she might accidently
touch us.

The Invitation

'You guys planning on going to study hall?'
Yasmeen asks.

We shrug simultaneously.
We don't even know what study hall is.

'Cool,' Yasmeen continues.
'Let's skip it and go to church.'

'Church?' Tippi says.
'I don't think so.
Not really our sort of thing.'

Jon grins.
'Well let's give it a try.
We might convert you.'

Baptism

When we were four months old
Mom took us to the vicar
who gulped when he saw us
and said,
'I'll . . .
        eh . . .
                have to
                check with a higher authority about
                whether we can baptise them
                separately.'

Mom never set foot
in a church again.

And neither did we.

Until today.

The Church is a Beautiful Ruin

It is a collection of stones and rocks tossed around
        like children's building blocks
        with a great abandoned bell lying
        beneath what was once
        its tower.

To get here we creep behind
the science labs,
down broken paths and
through a forest
of flies and brambles.

The Church sits next to
a pond littered with lily pads
and is the sort of place I imagine
fairies lurk,
or serial killers,
though Yasmeen says,
'Don't worry,
we won't get murdered.
We've been coming here for years
and no one else knows about it.'

'We'll just have a smoke today
and die that way,' Jon says,
and
takes such a pleasurable drag
from his cigarette you'd think he was
sucking up gold.

And soon they are both puffing away
like old pros.

Yasmeen blows a mouthful of smoke into the sky
then passes me her cigarette.

I shake my head but before I can object,
Tippi has the smouldering cancer-stick
between two fingers and is
inhaling great gulps
of tobacco and tar.

She stops
and coughs
so hard I think she might throw up.

Yasmeen laughs.

Jon scratches his head.

And I gently pat my sister
on the back
when what I really want to do is
let her choke.

Coffee and Cigarettes

I am a peppermint tea sort of person.
Tippi drinks coffee the colour of coal.
She guzzles down around five mugs a day
—not that I get a say—
as the caffeine careens around her body
and has her buzzing like a blender
     —and me, too
     these days.

It started as a milky latte to help get her going
in the mornings.
Then it was one at lunch
and another later
and before she knew it,
Tippi was a slave to the stuff.

So although
I know it's
just one
cigarette,
and
one cigarette
never killed a soul,

I also know Tippi.

Perhaps

'How did your day go?'
Mrs James wants to know
during our
debrief in her office.
'Do you think you could be happy
at Hornbeacon?'

'Happy?'
Tippi asks,
her head
        tilted to the side
        as though
she's never heard the word before
and is requesting a
translation.

'Happy,'
Mrs James repeats,
        waving jazz hands at us.
'Do you like it here?
Will you be staying?'

Tippi looks at me and
I smile.
'Perhaps,' she says,
and then again,
'Perhaps.'

We Wait

Long after
the other students
have gone home,
long after Yasmeen has waved goodbye
and promised to meet
us in the common room
tomorrow morning,
we wait.

It's past four o'clock by the time
Dad's car appears,

      mounting the curb and
      skidding to a stop.

      We creep out of our hiding spot between a
        clump of trees
but Dad isn't at the wheel.

Thank God.

He's slumped in the passenger seat,
his face as purple as a pickled beetroot.

Grammie is driving.

'He's hammered, isn't he?' Tippi says
as we slide into the backseat.

'Blotto!' Grammie says.
She stabs Dad
        with her fake fingernails
        and turns on the windshield wipers
        though it isn't raining.
'He didn't get the job
he interviewed for
yesterday,' she says,
like that's an explanation,
like Dad deserves our sympathy,
like lately he's needed an excuse
to be drunk.

Tippi and I are fidgety,
desperate to tell someone
about our first day,
that it wasn't perfect but
no one called us devil's spawn
or asked how many vaginas we have.

But we stay silent in the back seat
because if Dad wakes up
we'll have to listen
to his drivel
instead.

And no one,

no one,

wants
that.

Other Reasons

Grammie puts Dad to bed,
turns on the TV,
and settles in for the night,
a whole menu of prerecorded
programs ahead of her.

Dragon is in her room
dressed in a leotard and ballet slippers
staring at herself in a full-length mirror.
She dips and dives,
her body a fountain.

'He's always wasted,' she says,
stopping to sip
at a glass of water.

He is.

It's true.

But what can we do
except try to be perfect
and hope it'll keep him happy
and sober—
which it never does.

'So . . .' Dragon says,
'How did it go?'

'It was great,' I say aloud,
finally.

Tippi and I
flop down on to Dragon's bed
even though we should be
getting started on the dinner.

'We're definitely staying,' Tippi says
and I nod.

Jon creeps
        into my mind—
his nut-coloured eyes and star-lined hands.

I shake him away,
this boy I just met,
this boy I hardly know
because
he can't be why I like Hornbeacon.

I need other reasons.

I need other reasons
or I'll go mad with
longing.

No One Mentions

We eat baked potatoes for dinner,
crunchy shells with fluffy innards
that we smother in butter, grated cheese and tuna.

Mom asks about school but she
isn't as interested as we'd expected—
                                    or hoped.

She eats slowly and
stares at the tiny bubbles tiptoeing their way
to the top of her sparkling water
while Dad lies in bed,
stinking up their white sheets,
sleeping off the whiskey.

No one mentions the spare baked
potato getting cold in the oven.

No one mentions the stench of vomit
wafting up the hall.

We keep our voices low,
our mouths full,
and hope that tomorrow will be
different.

Selfish

'We have to talk about The Church,' I say
as Tippi and I lie
        side by side
        in bed.

'You're upset about the cigarette.
God, Grace.'
She sighs
and I feel
for a moment
so much
younger than her.

'I think we should have discussed it,' I say,
not needing to remind her
that
        this shoddy body
        never split like it should
        and that if she dies,
        so do I.

'Sorry,' she says.
        'So can I smoke?'

I turn my head,
        curl away from her
as best I can.

It isn't really a question:
When Tippi wants something
        she takes it with
        two hands
        and
        with a body that belongs to
        us both.

I know this should make me
angry,
but
all I feel is envy
because I so wish
I
could be more selfish
sometimes
too.

Naked

I shampoo my hair and
leave conditioner on the dry ends
for a few minutes
while Tippi scrubs herself down with a sponge
and wild lavender
body wash.
I lean away from the strong smell
so she won't get any suds on my arms or face
then
step under the water jet
and use a fresh bar of almond soap
to rub myself clean.

'Isn't it weird to see each other naked?'
our twelve-year-old
cousin Helen asked
last year
over Thanksgiving turkey,
which made Grammie
gag on a roast potato.

Tippi and I shrugged,
shook our heads
while everyone waited for an answer,

pretending they weren't,
and Tippi said,
'When you share a life,
seeing your sister's boobs
doesn't really feel like a
big deal.'

The First Fall

We are rushing to get ready,
        brushing our teeth,
        me with my right hand,
Tippi with her left,
our spare arms wrapped around each other's waists
like fishhooks.

And suddenly the mirror
disappears and
so does Tippi.

When I Wake Up

I am on the bathroom floor listening to the sound of
screeching,
Tippi shaking me back into the world.

She sighs
when I blink
and squeezes me.
'I'm OK,'
I manage
as
pounding feet beat against the hardwood floor
in the hall.

Dragon is at the door,
a blusher brush in hand,
which she is waving like a wand
and shouting,
'What the hell happened?'

'I slipped,' I whisper.

'Really?' Dragon asks,
hands on hips,
looking like Mom.

'Yes,' I lie, 'I slipped,'
and hanging on to the sink,
drag myself and Tippi up from the cold,
beige
bathroom floor.

Dragon is frowning.

'She slipped,' Tippi says.

Looking for Dragon

Dragon douses herself in candy-scented perfume
and has started wearing lipstick.
'You have a boyfriend, don't you?'
I say,
teasing her,
      wondering,
            hoping.

'Sort of,' Dragon says.

Tippi stops spreading cream cheese on a bagel
and gives Dragon serious
side-eye.
'It's cool if you don't want him to meet us.'

Dragon is wrapping a silky scarf tightly around her
  neck.
She pauses.
'It's not what you think.'

Tippi snorts.
'It's OK, really.
We get it.
We get what we are.'

Every feature of Dragon's face pinches together
  tightly.
'Yeah, I know who *you* are, too.
But who am I apart from your sister?
Can you tell me that?'
She ties the scarf in place
and waits.

We watch her.

'No, I didn't think so,' she says,
and storms out
slamming every door
behind her.

Reality

Taped to Tippi's locker is a note:
> *Why don't you*
> *go back to the zoo???*

Yasmeen grabs the paper,
scrunches it
into a tight ball,
and launches it
along the hallway.
'Assholes!' she shouts.
> *'You're* the animals!'

Students with books in their arms
lean on lockers and against one another.
They stare
wide-eyed and
> open-mouthed,
glad for an excuse to ogle us unhindered.

I knew it was way too much
to ask everyone to accept us—
or even to leave us
> alone.
Yesterday was a fluke and today
reality has arrived.

Yasmeen says,
'They're afraid of you,
like they're afraid of me.
We're different
and that's bad.'

Tippi stops us and squints.
'Why are they afraid of *you*?'
she asks Yasmeen,
her voice a spiky challenge.

Yasmeen turns.
'I have HIV,' she says, quite simply
and
tucks tiny strands of hair behind her heavily
   studded ears.
'I reek of death,
of low life expectancy. Like you guys,
I guess.'

'Yes,' we say in unison
and head for geometry to work on problems
a lot less complicated
than our own.

In Geometry

'But how do they know?'
Tippi asks
Yasmeen.
We are supposed to be correcting
each other's answers,
talking through the equations we
got wrong.
Mr Barnes, the teacher,
isn't even in the room.
He left
after setting us the task and hasn't come back.

'*I* told them.
I didn't think it would matter,' Yasmeen says.
'But the thing is,
it isn't like cancer.
With HIV
people think you've only got yourself to blame,
right?
Well,
I refuse to justify myself by
explaining
how I got it.

Screw that
and
screw them.'

How?

Yasmeen still hasn't asked us
the questions
which most people blurt out
within minutes of meeting us:
'Couldn't you be separated?'
        and
'Wouldn't you want to *try*?'

What people really mean is that
they'd do
anything
not to live like us,
that finding a way to look
normal
would be worth
any risk.

So even though all I want to ask
Yasmeen is *how, how, how*
on earth
she ended up with HIV,
I will not be the one to ask.

Remnants of Him

'Bastards,' Jon says
when he hears about the note
on the locker.

Tippi tickles her own armpits
and *oo-oo-oos*
like a monkey
until we laugh
and the malice of the message
has been boiled away
                    a bit.

We should be in study hall again
but are at The Church
sharing a bag of salted pistachios
and a bottle of cider.

I give Tippi narrow-eyed evils
when she takes a big swig straight
from the bottle
and fold my arms
over my chest to show my disapproval.

The smell of the booze
makes me think of Dad unsteady and angry
and I don't want any
part of that.

But then Jon takes a turn
and passes it to me.

I can't resist.

I put my lips to the rim
        and taste the remnants of him on it,
the closest I've ever come to being kissed.
And I sip until
        my head swims
while everyone else
        blows smoke rings
into the air.

Then we do animal impressions,
mewing and cooing and *oo-oo-ooing*,
turning The Church into
our very own zoo.

'Seriously, the note was stupid,' Jon says.
He takes the bottle from my hands
and guzzles down the last dribbles.

I shrug, try to look
                    unruffled.

'Hatred's better than sympathy,' I say,
and play with the ends
of my hair,
willing Jon
to keep
his pity-free eyes
on me.

Not Fair

Dragon drops her dance bag in the hall
and slumps on to the sofa.

'I didn't realise you were taking classes on Tuesdays,'
  I say,
putting down the book I'm reading.
Tippi looks up and mutes the TV.

'I'm teaching the little ones
in exchange for my own lessons,'
Dragon says. 'Didn't I tell you?'

'No,' Tippi and I say together.
'We didn't know that.'

We watch the silent screen,
the characters' mouths
        opening and closing,
their desires lost on us.

Mom comes into the sitting room.
'There's ravioli on the stove, Dragon,' she says.

'Did you know Dragon was working?' Tippi asks.

Mom nods. 'No harm in her pulling her weight,
is there?'

'And what about us? Should we get jobs too?'
   Tippi asks.

'It's not the same thing,' Mom says.
'Don't make this into an argument about your
   equality.'
She grabs the remote and laughter from the TV
         fills the room.

But Mom doesn't understand:
Tippi isn't angry that we aren't working;
she's pissed off that our little sister
has to.

Changing

In the overheated locker room during a free period,
we change for P.E. early so we don't have to strip
in front of a gaggle of girls.

Not that we'll take part
like the rest of the class—
we will join them for warm up stretches
and the wind-down walk.
We will
        sit out
the soccer game.

Yasmeen pretends to be texting
and doesn't look up as we
unbutton
our shirts.

We are sitting in our bras
taking a breath
when the door
        swings open
and the most beautiful girl in the whole school,
Veronica Lou,
bounds in

like an excited Labrador,
her shiny black hair
bouncy behind her.
She peers at us and stops,
holds her bag
up
like a shield and says,
'I thought I heard the bell.'

Yasmeen picks at her teeth.
'Next period starts in five minutes, Ronnie,' she
  says,
and Veronica nods
quickly,
      furiously,
backing out of the locker room
like she's just seen a monster.

Dessert

Grammie is late
so we head for ice cream,
Jon and Yasmeen pressed up close behind us.

It isn't like New York City here
or even Hoboken
where people are used to seeing oddballs:
the man who rides his bike
  dressed like Batman,
the obese belly dancer
  on the corner of Park and Sixth,
and us,
the glued-together twins
  who hobble around
on crutches
  clutching each other.

In Montclair we are new and
unexpected.

But still,
we try to focus,

        our hands
    pressed against the freezer glass,
        our eyes
    on rainbow rows of ice cream.

I want vanilla yoghurt.
Tippi chooses coconut cream
with chocolate chips.

Tippi and I share a lot
—we always share dinner—
but rarely,
if ever,
a dessert.

The Worst Thing

Slurping up the last of my frozen yogurt,
I overhear someone say,
'Being a Siamese twin has got to be
The Worst.
Thing.
Ever.'

And no one laughs
because it's not a joke.
It's just meant to be very sad and
very true.

Yet
I can think of
        one hundred things
worse than
living alongside Tippi,
than living in this body
and being who
I have always been.

I can think of a thousand things worse.

A million.

If someone asked.

Tragedy

I would hate to have cancer.
I would hate to have to get hooked up
to a machine every week
so they could pump poison into me
in the hope it would save my life.

Our uncle Calvin died of heart disease at
thirty-nine
leaving behind three sons and a pregnant wife.

Grammie's sister drowned in a barrel
of rotten peaches and stagnant water
when they lived on a farm
as little girls.

On the news are stories about
child abuse and famine and genocide and drought
and I have never once thought
that I would like to
swap my life for any belonging to those people
whose lives are steeped in tragedy.

Because having a twin
like Tippi is
not
The Worst
Thing
Ever.

Again

Dad comes back from another interview
and doesn't talk.

He sits with Grammie watching
Law and Order
and drinking warm beer.

After three bottles he storms out
and doesn't come back for hours,
not until he is red-faced and fizzing.

'Someone make me a sandwich,'
he commands,
leaning against the kitchen table.

Dragon jumps up
from her homework
to do it.

'Ham?' she asks.

Dad ignores her and sits on the sofa.

He is asleep before
she has even buttered the bread.

For Myself

Dr Murphy wants to know what happened in school,
so I tell her about the first week.
I talk about the pretty girls
in my class,
the lazy teachers,
and about Yasmeen's pink hair.

But I never mention Jon.

I keep Jon to myself.

Blood

Tippi and I are teaching Grammie how to
tag herself in online photos
when the blood comes.
We plod into the bathroom
and
I smile at the rust-coloured spot
as I do whenever this happens,
each time it's proven
that I am a real girl.

Dragon is in her room
        doing the splits.
'Got any sanitary pads?' Tippi asks.

Dragon
        leaps up
and pulls a full packet of pads from her closet.
'Have them,' she says,
and hurls them at us.

Tippi catches the pads.
'Won't you need them?'

'I don't think so,' Dragon admits.

I glance at the place on Dragon's body where a baby would
show itself,
but that's not it.

'What's wrong?' I ask.

Dragon flicks her hair over her shoulders.
'You guys aren't regular.
Must run in the family.'

But that is
not it
either.

What Is Possible

'Conception *is* possible,' Dr Derrick said
three years ago
when our first period came.
'But carrying a baby to full term
in conjoined uteri
would certainly
kill you
or
the baby.'

This is his professional opinion.

Then again,
he told Mom
we wouldn't see our second birthday.

Yet
here we are.

Sexy

'I like the way you say "squirrel," ' Jon says, laughing.

'How do I say it?' I ask.

We are in the common room
next to an open window.
Tippi and Yasmeen are
watching YouTube clips of Simon Cowell's worst
  insults
and no doubt
committing them to memory.

Jon pulls the straw from his carton of juice
and drags on it like it's a cigarette,
then blows imagined smoke
through the window.
'I don't know.
You say it like it's two syllables.
"Squir–rel," ' he says.

'It *is* two syllables,' I tell him.
'*Squir-rel. Squir-rel.*
Yes, definitely two syllables.'

'Nope.
It's one.
It's one long, sexy, nut-eating word.
Squirrel.'

It comes out of his mouth like
squeeerl
and then
it's my turn to laugh.
'You *have* managed to make it
sound
sort of sexy.
I admit that.'

He sucks on the end of the plastic straw again.
'Not hard.
I mean, if you use your whole mouth to speak,
your tongue and teeth and lips,
most words *are* sexy.
Especially the word *sexy*.
Sex-y,' he says, slowly.
And again,
'Sex-y.
Try it.
Use your whole mouth.'

He doesn't laugh.
He is watching me.

'Sex–y,' I whisper.

'Sex–y,' he says.
'Yeah.'

Driver's Ed

The instructor stutters as she explains
how cars work
—what the pedals do and where the indicators
  are—
but when I aim the key at the ignition,
she grabs my wrist.
'I h–h–honestly don't know how this will work.
How can you coordinate your feet
quickly enough to avoid cr–cr–crashing?
I can't understand it.'

And that's the thing.

People don't understand
our synchronicity,
the quiet connection
        that flows between us.

'Everyone knows that
ninety percent of communication
is nonverbal,' Tippi says,
and
while the instructor thinks about this,
I start the engine.

Train Ride

We are tired of getting rides
to school and back again every day
so we take the train home
with Jon
and pretend we can't hear all the words around us
like little waspy stings.

'I bet celebrities don't even have it this bad,' Jon
   says.
'I can't imagine what it must be like
for you.'

'It's like *that*,' Tippi tells him
and points at
a woman across the aisle with a phone
aimed at us like a sniper rifle.

'Want me to say something?'
he asks.

'No,' I say quickly
because
I do not want a scene
and
I definitely do not want
Jon to save us.

The Phone Call

'I got the job this time,' Dad says.
'I definitely got it.'

He sets a pizza box
down on the kitchen table
along with a bag of
sodas
and for once,
as a family,
we eat together,
telling each other
about our days,
mainly listening to Dad,
hearing how the director of Foley College
in the city
'loved' him
and 'practically' offered him a teaching job on the
    spot.

Mom clears the plates.

Dad's cell phone rings.
'Yes. Yes. OK.
I understand.
Thanks.
Yes. OK. Yes.'
Dad studies his phone
then fires it across the room.
It hits the wall
and smashes,
bits of black plastic and glass
raining down on the kitchen countertops.

'Another job will come along, son,'
Grammie says,

and Dad replies,
'Don't patronise me, Mom.'

It is the last thing he says
for three whole days.

Hitchcock

Three crows land in the yard
and peck at our tiny square of lawn.
They are joined by a magpie who
scowls at us through the patio doors.
Tippi points. 'Not good,' she says.
Tippi is not superstitious,
but she's an Alfred Hitchcock fan
and squirms at the sight of more than one bird.
She caught the bug from Mom and Dad, who
   started dating
the same week a Hitchcock season opened at Film
   Forum in
New York City.
They snuggled together
in the back row
on red velvet seats for two weeks
becoming Hitchcock experts and
falling in love.
So when they found out we were twins
it was a no-brainer to name us
after two of Hitchcock's biggest stars,
Tippi Hedren and Grace Kelly,
who were so beautiful it sometimes feels like a cruel
   joke.

But in any case, Tippi loves Hitchcock
and has seen every one of his movies.
So while I make notes on the Whitman poems
we were given for homework,
Tippi watches *Psycho* and mouths Vera Miles's lines
telling me not to worry about her or the
assignment,
that she'll read the SparkNotes online
and be just fine.

Preparing for an Apocalypse

A hurricane threatens
    the East Coast
    and we are sent home early from school.

The weather reporters warn that
the storm will bring
flooding and power outages,
so we prepare our
    ground floor apartment
for an apocalypse.

Dad clears the patio,
    puts everything in the hall,
Mom piles sandbags
    by the backyard doors,
and Grammie sends Dragon to the store
for canned fruit and toilet paper,
then makes Tippi and me
fill the tub and every jug we own
with water
just in case.

Maybe I should be worried,
but I'm just disappointed
that the weather is stopping us
from being at The Church with Yasmeen and Jon
where I feel
      free to breathe.

'Can we go to the waterfront?'
Dragon asks,
and Dad barks back an angry
'No,
it's dangerous, dammit.'
Maybe he's trying to be caring,
but he has a crappy way of showing it.

And so with nothing else to do
we watch out the window
with Dragon
and wait for the
      great tide
      and furious winds
      to devour our city.

In The Dark

Tippi is snoring
next to me
while the wind whirls and whistles outside,
and I want to get up and see what's happening,
but I'm too scared to wake her
in case she screeches,
complains she can't get back to sleep.

So I lie quietly
and listen
and try to imagine what the
hurricane is like,
and how it might be
to get up and look
out our bedroom window
all by
myself.

Palpitations

I do not know what I dream,
what the nightmare is,
but it wakes me
and I find myself
panting,
my heart palpitating,
my head a fog of grey words and swollen pictures.

Tippi opens her eyes.
'You all right?' she croaks.

'Yes,' I tell her.
'Go back to sleep.'

The View from Hoboken

Before the city is quite awake,
Tippi and I slog
up to Stevens Institute,
the highest point in Hoboken,
to look down at New York City
across the river
and see for ourselves
how resolutely rooted to
the ground the skyscrapers have remained.

All is as it should be:
The Empire State Building is standing up straight
and Chelsea Piers is
already open for business,
the golfers slamming balls
against high-rise nets to stop them
dropping into the Hudson River
and sinking
down
down
to the bottom.

'I guess the hurricane changed its mind
about visiting New York,'
Tippi says.
'I don't blame it.
That city stinks.'

And she turns away
to head down the hill,
pulling me toward
home
and breakfast.

Storm Apples

The only damage the storm managed was to
rip a ton of ripened apples
from the tree in the middle of our yard.
Now they're lying on the grass
like forgotten red billiard balls on green felt.

I'd been trying to
      knock them down for days
—banging a broom on the branches
and throwing
Dad's football at the biggest of them—
the ones highest and fattest and really red.

Tippi never helped.

She hates baking and knew that's all we'd do
if I managed to get any down.

She huffed and yawned and said,
'Can we go inside now, Grace?'
until we did just that.

Now all the apples are
a bit bruised and traumatised
      but OK
      for pie.

Tippi says,
'You know we could buy pie for a few dollars at the
store and save ourselves hours.'

Which isn't the point.

I want to hear the clean slice of
a sharp knife through the apple's flesh.

I want to roll the pastry flat and lay
it over the filling like a friendly blanket.

I want to watch the clock
and check the oven
and feel anxious about the results.

'Can't you pretend to be pleased?' I ask,
and Tippi sniffs.

'I can *pretend*,' she says,
which is a lie:
I'd be asking too much
for Tippi to pretend
anything,

        ever.

Pie

Dragon spends her free day at the dance studio.
Mom heads into work.
Grammie goes downtown to see a friend and
Dad just disappears.

We are alone
with nothing to do.

So.

Reluctantly
Tippi makes the flaky pastry
while I core, peel, and slice the apples,
and together we bake a pie
stuffed with cinnamon and sugar and definitely
better than anything you could
buy in a store.

When Tippi tastes it,
she concedes—a little:
'It's good,' she says,
pouring cream over her portion
and snaps a picture to post online

so everyone can see what we've done
with the flotsam from the storm.

Tippi looks into her licked–clean plate
and then at her phone as it buzzes.
'Yaz liked the picture of the pie,'
she says.
The phone drones again.
'And Jon, too.'

'Great,' I say quickly,
and serve myself another slice,
wondering what I was doing
when Tippi friended them online.

Beautiful

Jon is
        leaning in
        toward Yasmeen
and doesn't see Tippi and me
come into the common room
and perch
        behind the piano
on an unsteady stool.

I suck up the
last dregs of my green smoothie through a
straw and the slurp
almost drowns out
what Jon is saying.

But not quite.

'It's shitty because they're so damn pretty,' he says.
'What a waste.'

Yasmeen looks up and flushes all the way
from her collar bones
to the tips of her silver-studded ears,

so we are in no doubt
who they are talking about.

Tippi stands, dragging me with her,
kicking the stool away
and shouting:
        'A waste?
        We're a *waste*?'

Fury boils our blood and
our bodies pulse with rage.

Jon stands up, too,
tries to take my hand
but I pull away and glare at him,
daring him to say it again
or to defend his words
with ones that would be just
as hurtful.

'I didn't . . .
I didn't mean . . .'
His voice is quiet,
his eyes
hard and defiant.

'All I mean is that you're beautiful,'
he says.
'That's all I mean.'

I want to believe him,
talk to him,
let him
say more,
but Tippi
     drags me
     along the hall
     to hide in a classroom.

And I hate it.

I hate hiding here
where I normally feel
safe.

'I thought they were different,
but they're just as ignorant
as everyone else,' Tippi says.

I don't respond.

All I can
hear in my head is the word
beautiful
and it's as much as I can do not to
weep
      with joy.

Yasmeen's Explanation

We weren't gossiping
we were just saying how happy
we are you're both at Hornbeacon

and we weren't wishing you were any different
we were just saying how hot you are

come on we wouldn't hang around with you if
we didn't think you were cool
we hate almost everyone here but we don't hate you
and coming from us that's a fucking miracle

so stop being moody and let's go to
The Church for a smoke.

Jon's Apology

Yasmeen explained why I was wrong.

And I promise it was me who said it,
    not her.

But I'm so sorry if I made you sad,
    even for a second.

Because I didn't mean anything by it.

And I think you're both perfect.

But I know how it sounded.
And I want to be friends.
So please forgive me.
And let me make it up to you.

Because the only
    waster is me.

But
I meant what I said.

You're beautiful.

You know that,
don't you?

Punishment

Tippi and I work with each other in class,
away from all the other students
including Yasmeen and Jon.

During free periods
we stay away from the common room
and wander around the school grounds
looking for somewhere to sit
without getting stared at.

At lunch
we fend for ourselves in the cafeteria
and take our trays out to the quadrangle,
where we eat on a bench and watch
grey squirrels
scampering up and down
the chestnut trees.

We don't go to The Church
during study hall.
I use the time to draw little stars along my fingers
with a Sharpie
and Tippi cleans out her backpack.

In the halls between lessons Jon tries to talk to me,
grabs my arm and whispers rushed apologies.

Yasmeen sends Tippi one hundred texts.

But we stick to our guns.

We stay really mad at them
until it's pretty obvious that
they aren't the only ones being punished.

Skyward

Dragon is in an amateur production of *Swan Lake*.

She is playing the Swan,
dressed first in
      wispy layers of white netting
      all puffed up like a French pastry
and then from
head
to
toe
in raven frills and feathers.

At the theater,
sitting in the back row
where no one can leer at us,
I am mesmerised by her feet,
by the black ballet slippers bound to her
and how they
seem never to touch the stage.

I am mesmerised by Dragon's
legs and arms
and the way she can spin

and hold herself up so
high she seems suspended in the air—
not a galumphing dragon at all but a
dragonfly,
a butterfly,
a bee.

I am amazed and for a moment
I am jealous
because before *Swan Lake*
I never knew
that this is what other people
could do
if they only took the time
to train—
  I never knew that normal people
  could fly.

Out of the Spotlight

After the show
     Dragon poses for pictures
and hordes of proud parents
huddle together
holding out their phones
and snapping photos.

But Mom and Dad
have vanished.

'Where did they go?' I ask Tippi.

'Dad went to get the car,' she says.

We shuffle toward the stage
but by the time we reach it
we are too late:
the group is breaking up.

Dragon is already out of
     the spotlight.

thin

At Malibu Diner on Washington Street
where we all go for a celebratory dinner
after *Swan Lake*,
Dragon says,
'I want to dance *Romeo and Juliet* with Nureyev.'

'Who?' I ask.
My family dive into a plate of nachos.

'Oh, no one. Nureyev is dead
so there's no chance of dancing with him.
But he was the greatest in history.'
Dragon nibbles
like a gerbil
on the edges of a taco
and I notice, suddenly,
how skinny her fingers have become—
        like twigs with knots for knuckles.

'You're so thin,' I say,
taking her wrist and wrapping my
thumb and forefinger too easily around it.

Mom orders more soda.
Dad another beer.
Tippi is tucking into her taco.

'I know,' Dragon says,
and flushes,
        quite delighted
        by what she sees
        as a compliment.

A Joke

Dragon is teaching us the five basic ballet positions,
letting us use chairs for balance but
tipping a ruler against our backs to get them
  straighter
and under our chins to lift them.

Tippi and I haven't exactly got
the bodies of ballerinas
nor the discipline
and end up giggling so hard we topple over.

And she is laughing and laughing
until she realises that I am not—
that I can hardly breathe,
that every ounce of air
seems to have been sucked from the room.

Dragon shrieks and runs.

By the time Mom and Dad have arrived
Tippi is panting, too.

I pull her up.
I pull her up and face our parents.

'It was a joke,' I say.
　　　'I'm fine. I was *joking*.'

Dragon squints.
Mom and Dad frown.
But for some reason
everyone decides to believe me.

Everyone except Tippi.

OCTOBER

A Victory

Mrs Buchannan teaches the whole class badminton
and rather than watching,
we join in
awkwardly.
Still. Though the shuttlecock is light
and Tippi and I are given a
racket each,
we can't get close to beating a single player on the
  other
side,
even when that player is Jon,
even when he doesn't once run.

You'd think he'd let us win
a few points.

You'd think he'd do it as a mercy,
magnanimously letting the shuttlecock
drop on to his side of the court a couple of
  times.

But pity is not part of the game.

Maybe we should feel downhearted.
Maybe badminton should make us feel like losers.

But knowing we've lost fairly,

knowing Jon doesn't care how we take it,

that's a victory all in itself.

After Badminton

The victory feels pretty short lived
when
Tippi and I are forced to sit on the toilet seat
long
after gym class,
long after we've finished peeing,
just to get
our breaths back.

'We should take it easier,'
I say.

    'Yes, please,' Tippi agrees.

For once,
    she agrees.

Reunited

Tippi and I turn up at The Church
carrying a big bag of chips
for sharing.

'So we're all good again?' Yasmeen asks.

'Guess so,' Tippi says,
begrudgingly.

I smile.

I smile and Jon smiles
back.

'It felt like you were gone forever,' he says.

'I know,' I say.
'But we're back now.'

Normal

'Why aren't you friends with the jocks
or the rockers
or the nerds
or with *any* guys
at school?'
I ask Jon.

'I'm on a scholarship, Grace.
You know what that means.
We're too normal for them.'

'Are you kidding?
You are normal.
And normal is good.
Normal is my goal,'
I tell him.

He shakes his head and
takes my hand,
strokes my thumb
with his fingers
making the vessels in my heart burn.

'Around here normal is a slur,' he says,
'Deep down

everyone wants to be a
        star
and normal is the road to
        nothingness.'

But everyone is wrong.

Normal is the Holy Grail
and only those without it
know its value.

It is all I have ever wanted
and I would trade
weird or freakish or spectacular or astonishing
for normal
any day of the week.

'I love your normal,' I tell him,
then feel my face
burn up
as I wonder how I let
these words slip out—
words too close to the truth.

He watches me.

'I know you do,' he says.

The Reader

Jon lends me all the books he loves
once he's read them—
thick tomes like doorstops,
        corners curled down
        and spines broken and sun-bleached.

Sometimes I follow his lead,
read along in *The Grapes of Wrath*
        until I find a dog-eared page

then stop

so I can inhabit the rhythm of his reading,
feel how
it must have been for him to
        turn those pages,
see those words,
        trace the outline of his
        thoughts.

I cannot watch a film in secret,
and even with my headphones
on
I know that Tippi hears the tinny hissing

of my music
in her own ears.

But when I read,
        I am completely alone.
I have privacy from her
        and from everyone.

When I read
The Unbearable Lightness of Being
I am not in Hoboken but in
Milan Kundera's
        Prague
        with the seductive Sabina
who wears nothing but a bowler hat
and I am with her as she opens the door to her
art studio, where she welcomes her lover.

I am alone in Virginia Woolf's
Orlando,
        in Orlando's chamber
        when she wakes up a woman
after living her whole life a beautiful man.

And yet,
somehow,
knowing that Jon has run his eyes
along these pages
and digested the very same words
I am devouring,
makes me feel like
        I am tasting him, too.

Diet

I batter the chicken flat,
    flour it for schnitzel,
    and fry it in hot sunflower oil
until it
sizzles and
pops in the pan.

But the only thing to pass Dragon's lips
are a few slices of cucumber
from the undressed salad.
She nibbles at them like a baby rabbit
and slides everything else
    to the corner of her plate.

I put down my fork.

'You don't like the schnitzel,' I say.

Mom looks up and says,
'You have to eat, honey,'
though too tiredly to have any impact.

Dragon shakes her head.
'I had a huge lunch,'
she says, and smiles so hard,
                          and so wide,
        it can only be a lie.

Our Part

Dragon's ballet studio is planning a special six-week
  trip
to Russia,
but she can't go,
not when Mom and Dad are spending every spare
  cent
sending us to therapy and on the best health
  insurance
money can buy so
we don't
drop down
dead.

'It's Dad's fault,' Tippi says.
'Every time he drinks, he's flushing
money down the toilet.'

But we can't pretend that's all it is.
We have to own up to what we're costing—
to what we're making our sister sacrifice.

'You know what we could do,' I say.
Tippi waves away the
suggestion.

We've discussed being on TV before
and agreed not to do it,
agreed never to let anyone in
except those we love.

'Not a chance,' Tippi says.
'Not a chance in hell.'

When I tow Tippi into Dragon's room
our sister pretends she doesn't care about
going to Russia or about
the Bolshoi Ballet or about herself at all.

'I'll go another time,' she says,
then lifts one leg out behind her
        and using her desk as a barre
                bends her back
        into a perfect
lunula.

I could cry
but Tippi turns away.
'I won't be on TV,' she mutters.

Skinny

'Are you on a diet?'
Mom asks the next night,
opening a
can of salty salmon
and pinching Tippi's
forearm.

Tippi pulls away.

'Girls and their figures,'
Dad grumbles.
He hasn't been
drinking today.
He went into
New York instead,
so he smells clean
again,
      like wood chips
      and baby wipes.
But even so,
his voice is
      edged with spurs.

'We should see
Dr Derrick,'
Mom says.

She heaps the salmon
on to hunks of
wholegrain bread
and squirts
mayonnaise at it.

I look at Tippi.
She *has* lost weight
though I never noticed.

And it doesn't make sense.

I'm the one addicted
to carrot sticks and
fruity tea.

'Maybe we *should*
see a doctor,'
Tippi says, and I stiffen.

'Yes,
make an appointment,'
Dad tells us,
and stomps
out of the room
        leaving a trail
        of grey mood
        behind him.

'There's seriously no need,' I say. 'I feel great.
Don't you?'

Tippi tenses
and bites into her half of our
salmon sandwich.
'Most of the time,' she whispers.
'But not always.
And you don't, either.'

Searching for String

Dad buys a bird feeder,
that he fills with seeds.
He thrashes around in the junk drawer
for some string
to hang the long, green, three-storey cylinder
and when he can't find any
stomps down to the basement
coming up
minutes later
empty-handed.
The longer he searches for string,
the harder he treads,
the stiffer he breathes.

'Let's help him look,' I say.

Tippi shakes her head.
    'He's not a child,
    let him deal with his own goddamn feelings,'
    she says,
as though she hasn't figured out
that Dad's feelings are always
someone else's responsibility.

How He Is for Others

Before winter comes
        barrelling in with bared teeth and
        icy jaws,
Dad fires up the BBQ
and we get the whole family over
to eat hot dogs and blackened corn.
        'Your dad is *so funny*,'
        our cousin Hannah says,
        watching him
        and giggling
as Dad does his Beyoncé dance,
wiggling his butt,
spinning his arms,
and hanging off Mom like she's a human pole.

'He isn't always like that,' I say.

        'Really?' Hannah asks.

'*Really*,' Tippi says.

        Our cousin frowns and
        shakes her head;
        she doesn't believe a word of it.

Cankles

On Monday morning
Tippi and I sit
on a table in the common room
and watch Yasmeen and Jon scrambling
to copy down our answers for history
homework.

Tippi lifts her leg and points her toes.
'I have a chubby ankle,' she says.
'When did that happen?'

Yasmeen looks up,
prods Tippi's foot with the point of her pen.
'You're probably pregnant,' she says,
and smirks.

I laugh and lift my own leg.
Point my toe.
See that my ankle
isn't as slender as it used to be
either.

How is that fair?

For conjoined twins
to have cankles
as well as everything else?

When Apart

Now Jon and I have swapped numbers
and he is among
my Favourites
I spend any lessons
        apart from him
with my phone hidden
        beneath my desk
sending
messages and waiting for replies.

Tippi rolls her eyes.
'I won't let you cheat later,'
she says.

But I don't care.

There's another message coming through.

Texts

Wot do the tattoos on ur
hand mean????

Nada

Can't b nothing

Can

Can't

Mayb I like stars . . .
Mayb I'm that shallow

Ur not!

I am

Tell me!!!

They remind me the
universe is bigger
than me

Than u?

Than what we think should
matter

I need some stars 2

U totally do

On the Sidelines

The other girls play basketball
while we sit on the sidelines,
me with a book,
Tippi with her headphones in.

Margot Glass isn't doing gym
either
and sits with us,
right by me
on the wooden bench.

'Got my monthly,' she explains,
taking out a tube of sticky lip balm
and smearing it all over
her plump pink lips.

'Tic Tac?' she asks,
holding out a transparent box brimming
with tiny white capsules.

Our classmates have offered us nothing
but
        a wide   berth
so I'm surprised Margot is even talking to me.

'Sure,' I say,
and Margot
       rattles
       four tiny pieces of candy
       into my hand.

'I was saying to some of the other girls last
  night
how sorry I feel for you and your sister,' Margot
  says.
'I need my privacy.
I'd hate to be so trapped all the time.'
Margot
opens her mouth
and tips the Tic Tacs straight inside.

'It doesn't bother us,' I say.

Margot Glass almost smiles—
her lips and eyes
hard and mirthless.

I curl my fingers around the
Tic Tacs in my palm and
slowly
the sweet minty coating melts
in my sugary
fist.

Thank You Anyway

Jon's lawn is littered with empty beer cans and
a rusting, tyre-less bicycle is tied to the chain-link
   fence.
The windows of his house
are protected by bars
and his front door has green graffiti sprayed across
   the glass.

As he pushes open his door
a German shepherd leaps at us
and licks our arms.
         'Down, Pup,' he says,
and pulls the dog away.

The house smells of cigarettes.
Dirty dishes are piled high in the sink.
The TV is on—no one is watching it.

Jon goes to the refrigerator.
         'Coke?' he asks,
and I am filled up with shame
because the last thing I want to
do is eat or drink
anything in this house.

The doorbell buzzes.
        'That'll be Yasmeen,' Jon says, and
rushes to open it.

A guy with a grey beard and
        a teardrop tattoo below his eye
emerges from a bathroom door
        in the corner of the kitchen.

'Fuck me,' he says,
dropping a cigarette on to the tiled floor
and grinding it down into tobacco dust
with the heel of his boot.
'I mean . . .
        fuck me,' he repeats,
and
as sweetly as if we'd been offered
pumpkin pie,
Tippi replies,
'No.
But thank you anyway.'

In Jon's Room

Jon's bedroom smells of stale bedsheets
and aftershave.
The walls are covered with photographs of dead
  writers
        and
        tattoo art.

'Sorry I was rude to your dad,' Tippi says,
and then,
'though I'm not really sorry.'

Jon laughs.
'Cal's my stepdad. He's OK.
He's here, you know.
He stayed after Mom bailed.
And he's an asshole sometimes, but he didn't leave.
He pays for my train tickets and lunch,
and if it weren't for him
I'd be at that shithole school across the street
and never get out of this place.
Cal said he'll stick around until I go to college.
Then he's moving to Colorado.
He likes snow.'

Yasmeen lies back on Jon's bed and hums,
Tippi checks out his tower of DVDs,
and I watch Jon digging
under a mountain of creased up laundry,
wishing I had the courage to tell him
that his mother should have stayed,
he didn't deserve to be abandoned,
and
that
leaving him
was the stupidest thing
she ever did.

Well, It Can't Hurt Me

For my tenth birthday
Mom bought me a silver
rabbit's foot pendant.
Since then, I've not taken it off,
never let a day go by
that I didn't have luck
lying against my skin.

'What's that?' Jon asks,
turning the pendant
over in his fingers,
his hand smelling of soap.

'It's for luck,' I tell him.
He narrows his eyes,
moves closer to me on the bed.

Tippi and Yasmeen aren't listening.
They are looking at a takeout menu
and choosing pizza toppings.

'You really believe in that stuff?'
Jon asks.

I lower my gaze
feeling suddenly very young.
'I don't know,' I say.
'But it can't hurt, can it?'

'I don't know,' he says,
letting go of the rabbit's foot,
'I really don't know.'

Jealousy

Jon gives us a ride home
in Cal's car
and I have to work really hard
not to be mad at Tippi
for being the twin on the left
and sitting
so close to Jon
for a full fifteen minutes.

Waiting Up

Dad is lying on the sofa,
alone in the dark.

'You're very late,' he says.

'Sorry,' Tippi and I reply together.
We step towards him.

'I was worried,' he tells us.

The darkness eases.

'Well, you're home now,' he says.
'Good night.'

And without another word,
he slinks off to bed.

Anything But

Tippi fidgets in the bed next to me then
gets out her phone,
     its light
       bright on her face.

'Something on your mind?' I ask,
waiting for it,
whatever *it*
is.

She rolls her head
     to the side
and looks at me with a sad expression
that is mine.

'Oh, Grace,' she says.

She blinks with my eyes
and bites my lips.

We look so much
the same person
that sometimes I am repulsed
by her,

sick of staring into
a mirror
every day of my life.

'We can go to school,' she says,
'and get jobs
and drive and swim and hike.
You know I'll follow
you anywhere, Gracie.
Anything you want,
tell me,
and we can do it.
We can do anything,
OK?'

'OK,' I say.

'But we can never
        ever
        fall in love.
Do you understand?'

'Yes,' I whisper.
        'I understand.'

But her warning comes
        too late.

The Bunker Boys

The original Siamese twins,
Chang and Eng,
    Left and Right,
The Bunker Boys
as I like to call them,
were born with a band of cartilage
connecting them
chest to chest.

They were the poster children
for people like us—freaks, of course,
but successful ones
once they dodged King Rama's
death sentence
as babies.

And despite what Tippi says about love,
Chang and Eng Bunker
had two wives and twenty-one children
between them.

They lived, loved, fought,
and died together,

which gives me hope
and makes me wonder
what's stopping us
from being
a little Siamese
ourselves.

Word Association

'You seem distracted,' Dr Murphy says.

Tippi is listening to some new album.
Her foot taps out the beat.
I wish I were with her in the music
instead of here
with Dr Murphy who is doing nothing useful—
just trying to make
me
      feel.

'I'm good,' I say.
'I love the new school.'

Dr Murphy's eyebrows seesaw.
She puts down her clipboard and pencil.

'Let's play word association,' she says.

We've played this game before.
We've played this game and I've always
lied
because what could

any
one
word
tell her?
How could
one
word
show her who I am?

'Marriage,' she says.

Marriage:
Mom, dad,
bad, sad,
snapped, broken,
empty,
alone.

'Cake,' I say, and clap lightly like I think this is a
game and not a way for her to root around my mind.

Dr Murphy says,
'Sister.'

Sister:
here, now,
joined, blood,
bones, break,
faint, fall,
die,
alone.

'Dragon,' I reply.

Dr Murphy sniffs and I can't tell whether
that means I've passed her test or not.
It doesn't matter, though.
Our time is up
so no more
probing.

Not
until next time.

The Waterfront

Tippi and I walk uptown then
    east
to the waterfront
to meet Mom getting off the commuter
ferry from the city.

The Shipyard isn't like it was
years ago,
a home for metal workers and longshoremen,
a practical place of industry.

Nowadays it's overrun with
    juice bars and
    yoga studios,
pushchairs more expensive than cars.

The ferry docks.

I put my hand on the back of a bench,
shut my eyes,
pant like I've just run a marathon,
my
heart racing,

begging me to slow down.
'Grace?' Tippi says.

I open my eyes as
Mom appears on the
  wide gangplank
  and waves.
The boat spews black smoke into the
Hudson River.

I wave back and so does Tippi.
'All good,'
  I say,
  and we go together
  ready to meet our mother
  with a smile.

A Bit of Breathlessness

'Something isn't right,' Tippi says
on the train to school next morning.
'I don't want to go to Rhode Island
any more than you do.
But something's wrong.'

I hold her hand.
'It's just a bit of breathlessness,' I say.

'Right,' Tippi says.
'So you won't mind me mentioning it
to Dr Derrick at the next check-up.'

Saint Catherine

In philosophy we are
examining the mind–body argument
through the ages so we can
prepare for a debate.

And I am all about
Saint Catherine of Siena, born in 1347.
She survived the black death
as a baby,
though
died anyway at thirty-three because
she would not eat.

Tippi says it was undiagnosed anorexia
but Saint Catherine said she didn't believe
her soul needed that sort of nourishment
and focused,
instead,
on God and prayer,
on giving up on matter
and climbing a ladder to the divine.

Sometimes I wish I could be like that:
committed
to my soul
instead of worrying
about this body all the time.

EARLY NOVEMBER

A Surprise

Instead of wearing her green school skirt,
Yasmeen is in a denim mini
and a pair of leopard print pantyhose.
She's sprayed her
pink hair
up high
     into a cresting wave
and the teachers don't make her change because
today is her seventeenth birthday and everyone
  knows
birthdays
for the sick
are sort of sacred.

'I might have sex to celebrate,' she says,
and whoops so loudly
everyone in the art room
suspends their paintbrushes
     above their watery
     self-portraits
     to look at her.

Instead of a party
Yasmeen is having a sleepover.

That's what we tell Mom.

We don't tell her we'll be
squatting at The Church on Saturday
under bare branches
and blinking stars,
creeping around the school grounds
when it's locked up for the night.

Once Jon's gone to mix more paint,
Yasmeen passes us a card,
a glittery heart with the word
LOVE in swirly capitals
like a monogram
on the front.

'It's from Jon,' she says.
'I wish he wouldn't.
I've told him how I feel.'

My heart
        rams my ribs
like I've been
        hammered from
                behind on the dodgems.

I hand back the card without reading it.

Yasmeen's self-portrait is black,
the eyes tiny pebbles in a too-round face.
'Bad, isn't it?' she says.

I don't know whether she means
the portrait or the
Problem of Jon.

All I know is that
I can think of harder knocks
than being liked by him,
than opening a card
covered in his kisses.

'You're probably making too much of it,'
Tippi tells Yasmeen.
She opens her mouth
to add something
but changes her mind
and strokes my side instead.

'You all right?' Tippi asks later.

I nod.

I'm fine.

And then I say,

'I'm getting drunk at The Church.'

I Watch Him

I watch how he is with Yasmeen
but I can't see his love for her anywhere
and I wonder whether
she could be wrong,
whether the card
really means
what she suspects.

Either she is wrong,
or I am blind,
because from where I'm standing
I can't see that he treats us
any differently.

Eating for Two

I'm not hungry.
Even the sight of the peppered chicken
on a bed of yellow rice
makes my stomach turn.
I have to look away.
'You don't want that?'
Tippi asks.
     I push
     my small plate toward her,
my half of the serving.
'You have it,' I say,
and quickly she gobbles up
enough for the both of us.

More Important

Bruised clouds gather in the distance.
'I hope
it doesn't rain tonight
and stop us from going out for
Yasmeen's birthday,' I say.

Tippi tows me away from the window.
'Worrying won't help,' she says.

'Worrying won't help what?' Mom asks,
coming into our room,
        peering over the tower of clean clothes
she is carrying.

'Grace doesn't want it to rain,' Tippi says.

Mom puts down the clothes and picks up
two dirty plates
covered in crumbs.

'If I were you,
I'd worry about
something more important,' she says,
and without saying what that should be,

leaves the room
and carefully
closes the door behind her.

Palmistry

The Church is alive with the yipping and ticking
of night bugs.

The moon is hidden
    behind thick clouds.
A chill inches its way
    beneath my sweater and
into my bones.

I thought the beers I downed would quell
my feelings for Jon,
    chase them into a quiet place
and leave room for me to think of other things—
    things
    that would be
    possible.

But it's the opposite.

My head is fogged up with words I want to whisper
to him here in the darkness.

His face is more beautiful now than ever
and his laugh makes my muscles tighten with
  longing.

Tippi feels it, flinches,
then sips at an almost empty
bottle of red wine and nibbles on a hash brownie.

Yasmeen strums out some Dolly Parton
songs on a guitar and sings, too.

Jon is sitting next to me on the damp
log.
'Give me your hand,' I demand,
and take it,
turning
        it palm up
        to face the black sky.

        'Tell me my future,' he says.

I draw my thumb
                diagonally
across his palm
and stare at him in the moonshine,

absorb him
    and our closeness.
'Your head line shows you're curious and creative,' I
  say.
'And the heart line is strong.'

     'I see,' he says,
widening his fingers
and offering me his whole hand.

The beer is trying to bully me
into saying something I shouldn't.
I clamp my tongue between my teeth
until I taste blood.

Tippi shivers and pulls a blanket around her
  shoulders.

I jump and stare at her.
    'What?' she asks,
    'Did you forget I was here?'

She laughs
    and I look away
because

yes,
actually,

for a moment
    I had forgotten
    her.

The Gift Our Mothers Gave Us

We finish fortune-telling,
singing, drinking,
smoking, celebrating,
and are quiet.

Yasmeen breaks the
silence and says,
'My mom gave me HIV.
She didn't know. She just gave birth then
breastfed, and I didn't stand a chance.
I sucked that nasty stuff right out of her.'

No one replies
but I don't think Yasmeen needs us to.

A shooting star glitters across the slate-coloured
  sky
and I hold my breath and wish upon it—
sending all its good energy
                    Yasmeen's way.

Tippi takes my hand and nestles closer
because we know how Yasmeen feels,
how it is to be burdened at birth
by a curse your mother
never knew she was under.

Maternal Impressions

If we'd been born in another century
fingers would have been pointed and
questions raised about
what was going through Mom's
mind while we were growing inside her.
Back then they would have said
she'd been looking at
pictures of devils or reading satanic stories
while she was pregnant,
that the images had trickled
into her womb and
imprinted on our easily broken bodies.

      Back then, there would have been
someone to blame
and it would have been
      Mom.

Nowadays the scientists know that she
did nothing wrong,
that it wasn't her fault,
that our strangeness didn't leak out of Mom's
mind
like sewage into a clear stream

but was a simple accident at conception,
the ova
not separating like
it should.

This is science and progress
and it has to be a good thing,
but it makes me wonder
about the tests they've done
on Mom
to determine how it happened,
how we came to be,
and whether they could prevent
people like us from ever
being born
again.

In the Morning

We are stiff and sore
and our heads pound
with hangovers
so heavy that
even the plinking
birdsong is too
much to bear.

In spite of it all
        we are smiling
        and,
        I think,
I have probably
never been
so happy.

A Thing He Is Doing

The hallway is a cloud of dust.
Dad is up a stepladder sanding a spot on the wall.
'Hey there, girls!' he says,
and 'Careful of that can of paint,'
and, 'I thought I'd freshen up the place.
What do you think?'

'It's an ace idea!' Grammie shouts
from elsewhere.

Wallpaper pieces, torn and twisted,
are strewn on the floor
like fallen leaves.
It took Mom two weeks to put the paper up.
It cost her a fortune
and now Dad's pulling it all down.

'Where's Mom?
Does she know what you're doing?'
I am whispering.
I am so quiet the dust
doesn't move
in the air.

'It's a surprise,' Dad says.
He whistles
and gets on with the sanding.
'How was your night?'

I know he wants us to be excited because
this is
A Thing He Is Doing.
And I really want to cheer him on.

But.

Tippi coughs and covers her mouth.
'I think you should have told Mom,' she says.

Dad stops whistling.
'It's *a surprise*,' he repeats.
'Ever heard of one?'

'Yeah,' Tippi says. 'Thing is,
I always prefer to be happy than surprised.'

Hangover

We climb into bed
still wearing our dirty clothes from the night
before.
I try to read
but the words
      twirl
on the page
unable to find a
      secure spot,
so I listen to an audiobook instead
and rest my head on
my sleeping sister's shoulder.

Lucky Avocado

Grammie is going on a date with a man she
met she at the bowling alley.
I didn't know Grammie liked bowling.
I didn't know bowling alleys were places to meet
    men.
And I can't believe that someone
with a face as wrinkled
as an overripe avocado
has more luck
in love
than
I have.

Partners

When Mr Potter tells us to pair up
for the philosophy project,
Jon taps my arm and says,
'Wanna work together?'

Tippi sniffs.
    'Grace and I are sort of a pair already,'
    she says,
    'in case you hadn't noticed.'

Jon tuts and pulls me to him,
his fingers pattering my ribs
like piano keys.
'But I thought you were separate people,'
he says—
    testing her.

Tippi turns to her left and
taps Yasmeen's arm.
    'I guess it's you and me,' she says.

    Later Tippi says,
    'If you could choose between me and a boy,
    who would it be?'

'It's just a school project,' I say.

'I know *that*,' Tippi says,
laughing,
and out of the blue
punches me in the arm.

Live Forever Or Die Together

In English class
Margot Glass
reads out the poem she's written
called 'Love'
about a girl who is in
so deep
she wants nothing more than to
lie down
and die
with her lover.

Our classmates sigh and clap
and are in awe of Margot's
depth,
the passion in the poem.

However.

They look at Tippi and me,
our forever togetherness,
as a couple cursed.

So when we tell them
we do not want to be apart,
waking alone in the mornings
and spending long days looking for someone
to share them with,
they assume there is
something very, very
wrong with
us.

And Yet

Being with Jon makes
me wonder
for a few fleeting seconds
what it might be like
to pull away from Tippi
for just a moment
and have him see me
as I am,
a single soul
with
separate thoughts,
and not another person's
                        appendage.

Divided

'Sometimes I wish I could see myself
through your eyes,' Jon says.

We are pouring purple chemicals into test tubes
about to make them pop under the heat of a flame.

> 'How do I see you?' I ask,
> knowing the answer already
> and wanting desperately to tell him.

'When you look at me,
you see something whole,' he says.

He quickly cuts his hand through
the blue Bunsen burner flame.

> 'No one is whole,' I tell him.
> 'We're all missing pieces.'

Jon's eyes crinkle—
his mouth looks unconvinced.

'Plato claimed that
we were all joined to someone else once,' I say.
'We were humans with four arms
and four legs,
and a head of two faces,
but we were so powerful
we threatened to topple the Gods.
So they split us from our soul mates
        down the middle,
and doomed us to live
forever
without our counterparts.'

'I love Plato,' Jon says,
and then,
'So what you're saying is that
you and Tippi are the lucky ones.'

    'Maybe,' I say
    because I do not want to admit
            that my heart
    has been divided
    since I met him.

Expensive

Aunty Anne has had a baby—
a boy weighing in at seven pounds, two ounces.
I'm sure my aunt is thinking,
Oh God,
how on earth
will I ever pay for
all the food and clothes and college bills?

And sixteen years ago my parents were no different
except they
knew
they would never be able to pay
for everything we needed
and would
have to make do with
      handouts from well-wishers
if they ever wanted to eat again.

'Babies are worth every cent,'
Mom tells her sister on the phone,
opening a bill from Dr Murphy
and inspecting the balance
at the bottom.

But I'm not sure.

I'm not sure how much
lives like ours are
worth to the real world
and especially
to the insurance company which,
every day,
queries our need
for so much healthcare.

Redundant

Mom's company laid off ten people this morning:
　　bing–bang–gone.

By noon Mom thought she'd survived the slaughter
and went for lunch,
　　bought herself a sausage sandwich
　　and a giant oatmeal cookie—
　　her favourites.

When she got back,
Mr Black called her in to his office
and told her the bad news.
It's not her fault, apparently,
that they don't need her any more,
just a sign of the times,
very bad luck.

Then
Steve from security followed her to her desk
and watched her pack up her things
like she was a criminal about to abscond
with the office stapler.
She said goodbye to her friends,
the women she thought were her friends,

who didn't make eye contact as she
was led to the elevator
and through the revolving doors
in the glass building
to the street.

Now Mom is in bed crying.

No one can console her.

And very soon,
no doubt,
we'll be destitute.

Bargaining

I kick off my sneakers but

Tippi keeps hers on.

'You know he hates shoes in the living room,'
  I say.
I can't help my voice getting high,
sounding horribly like a schoolteacher.

Tippi pulls me down on to the sofa.

'What's he gonna do about it?' she asks,
and puts her foot up on the coffee table.

'I dunno,' I say. 'He'll be annoyed. He'll.
He'll . . .'
I stop,
        lean forward, and push her foot to the
floor.

Tippi turns to me.
'He'll drink no matter what we do, Grace.
You've got to start understanding that.
You can't bargain with him.'

She touches the silver rabbit's foot
hanging around my neck.
'Haven't you covered this with
your shrink yet?'

'I don't know what the hell
you're talking about,' I say,
    pulling away,
        tucking the pendant
        into my shirt
        to hide it.

'Yes, you do,' Tippi says,
and slams her foot
right back up
on the coffee table.

At Two A.M.

A door bangs. Pots clang.
A radio blares out
late-night symphonies
over curses and groans.

Dad is making himself a meal
now the rest
of us are in bed
trying to get some sleep.

'What's wrong with him?' I wonder aloud.

Tippi sniffs.
'Maybe he found out I didn't
take off my shoes.'

Cutbacks

It starts with no more nights out at the movie
  theatre,
no new clothes or money for restaurants.
It starts out with regular cutbacks
that none of us notice
all that much.

But
then it's no money for gas and no money for meat
and no money for any treats
or frittering
except healthcare
because
Mom
won't skimp
on that.

Contributions

Grammie sells a few old rings and things
on eBay
to keep us ticking along.
Mom spends long hours ironing for cash,
undercutting the women in the Laundromat,
earning hardly anything.
And a couple of nights a week
Dragon babysits our neighbour's
little boy.
Everyone is pulling their weight
except Dad.

Except Us.

'We have to help out,'
I tell Tippi.

'And what do you suggest?' she asks.

I push her bangs out of her eyes.
'You know how we could make
thousands without
giving up a thing,' I say.

Tippi sighs.
'If we went on television,
we'd be giving up
our dignity, Grace,' she says.
'And I won't let us lose that.'

But what's the point in saving your pride
when you've given up everything else?
That's what I want to know.

Adjournment

Dad helps Mom update her résumé and
they laugh loudly,
sitting side by side at the computer,
hands touching.

Maybe it means
they love each other again.
Maybe Mom losing her job
could be a blessing
instead of the curse
we all thought.

But then
Mom goes out.

She's only away a couple of hours,
but it's long enough for Dad
to forage for booze and
get blotto.

Tippi and I hide in our room
picking through homework handouts and
upcoming quizzes,

wishing Dragon weren't still at the studio
so we'd have a comrade to help
us see out the night.

But nothing happens.

We creep into the kitchen,
where Mom is sitting slicing lettuce.

'Everything OK?' I say.

Mom looks up and nips the tip
of her finger with the knife.

Bubbles of blood ooze on to the table
though she doesn't seem to notice.

'I'm making a Greek salad,' she says,
and we nod.

'I'll get the feta,'
Tippi says gently.

But Mom shakes her head.
'I didn't have money for feta,'
she confesses,
then puts her ring finger into her mouth
to suck away the blood.

Around Strangers

Mrs McEwan from upstairs stands in our doorway,
her son Harry
      balanced on her hip.
'Is Dragon home?' she asks,
looking at neither of us particularly.

I shake my head.
      Tippi says, 'She's at dance practice.'

Mrs McEwan sighs.
'Oh, what a shame.
Well, if she gets back soon,
will you tell her I came calling?'

I nod.
      Tippi says, 'We can watch Harry for you,
      if you like.
      We'd love to.'

Mrs McEwan swallows hard.
'Oh no. Oh no.
He's sort of nervous around strangers.'

The toddler grins
and reaches for one of my hooped earrings.
Mrs McEwan pulls him back
and laughs.

'Tell Dragon I called, OK,' she mumbles,
and scurries up the stairs
to her apartment
taking her precious
'frightened'
bundle
with her.

Easy Money

If I owned a pistol I could rob a bank.

I could stick a gun in a teller's face
and demand a stack of cash
then motor off in a stolen Maserati.

I could sell drugs to kids on street corners
or pimp out girls to the highest bidder.

I could break any law I wanted.

If they imprisoned me,
they'd have to lock up Tippi too,
which is false arrest,
illegal,
and would never stand up in a
court of law.

If I didn't have this damn conscience,
     we'd be rich.

Apologies

'I'm sorry,' Mom says,
    sitting us down on the bed
    so we won't storm off
    before she's had a chance to finish.
    'We're moving.
    We can't afford the apartment any more
    or the taxes to live in Hoboken.
    We can't even afford to pay the
    goddamn phone bill.
I'm sorry.'

'It's not your fault, Mom,' I say,
    trying to be kind,
    trying not to blame her for
    losing her job,
    or sending us
    to school in the first place
    and making us fall in love with it.

'I'm sorry,' she repeats.
    'We'll sell the apartment and buy
     something
    more affordable in Vermont.
    You have cousins there and

I'm sure the state
will find funding to send you
to another great school.'

'It won't be Hornbeacon,'
      Tippi says,
      unable to console our mother
      or concede.
      And this time I don't
      really blame her because
      she's right.
It won't be Hornbeacon.
It won't be Jon and Yasmeen.

Dragon's head appears around the door.
'It sucks,' she says,
      'But we'll be OK.'
      She is slouching,
      her shoulders hunched
            her head dipped
      so she looks completely unlike herself
      and not even half convinced
      by what she's saying.

'You'll have to give up your ballet studio,' I say.
'You might not find one you like in Vermont.'

Dragon shrugs.
Her eyes fill with water.

'I'll cope,' she says.
    'I'll dance on the ski slopes.'

I pinch Tippi's knee and she looks at me.
 'No,' she says firmly,

and after a pause,

'Maybe.'

Finally

Staring at our shoes
Tippi says, 'Call the reporter.'
Her voice is wispy
like laundry drying on a line.

'Call her,' she repeats,
'and let's get this fucking freak show started.'

Double Standards

'Are you sure about this?'
Dragon asks.
'I mean, you'd be paid for idiots to gawk at you.
Is that what you want?'

Gorgeous people strut down catwalks
in dresses made of string,
loll half naked on sandy beaches
and no one seems to mind
that they do this for money—
no one finds it
distasteful
at all.

But when Tippi and I consider cashing in on our
   bodies,
everyone frowns.

Why is that?

MID
NOVEMBER

Caroline Henley

She sips at the tea Mom's made
and chats about such ordinary things
you'd never know she'd been hounding
us for years
       —calls, emails, texts—
begging to be allowed
behind-the-scenes access to
our conjoined lives
so she can make
a full-length documentary.

'Bumpy landing,' she says,
sticking to the safe subject of her journey.
I've never heard a voice so
richly British and politely prim,
like she's travelled from the 1940s
and not just climbed off a flight from London.
'Hit the runway with such a
            thwack
I thought the wheels would
            fly off.
And the traffic on the highway.
Just dreadful!'
She drinks more tea.

'Hotel's lovely. View of the river,
Statue of Liberty.
I've never been to New York before.
So much to see.'

Mom offers Caroline another cookie.
'How many days are you staying?'
she asks.

Caroline coughs.
'You mean months,' she says.
She conjures up a contract
from inside her blazer,
slapping it down on the side table
like a ransom note.
'I'd want complete access the whole time.
Everything's here in black and white
for you to read and sign.
I've a pen,'
she says,
and supernaturally
        produces one of those.

Her eyes are suddenly hard and
brimming with ambition.
'People will want to see you at home,

school, shopping for clothes.'
She breaks a cookie in two
and pops one of the pieces into her mouth.
'I'm so glad to be here.'

Dad is sitting straight-backed and jiggling one foot.
He's promised to be good
while Caroline films our lives,
although that was before we knew
she'd be here so long.
He snaps up the contract,
scans it with bloodshot eyes.
'Wanna see them take a leak, too?' he asks.
'How about showering?
People might be curious.'

Caroline doesn't giggle like the rest of us,
as we try to smooth over the crinkles
in Dad's bad temper by pretending
he's joking.

She knows he isn't.

'Bathrooms are out of bounds,' Caroline says.
'But I'll follow them everywhere else.
And you'll *all* be on film.

There's another daughter
I believe,' she says, talking about Dragon
like she's a dog we own
and not our sister.
But we've already thought
of a way to get Dragon
out of the picture,
because no one's going to
make a mockery of her life.

Dad flicks through the contract,
pages and pages of clauses and disclaimers
none of us will ever decipher.
Mom is silent.
She does not want this.
She has always kept us
        hidden
and safe
and I can tell she's ashamed,
like she feels
she is selling us.

'When do they get their money?' Grammie asks,
not a jot of decorum
anywhere in sight.

Caroline's eyes shine.
'As soon as the contract's signed,'
she says,
        handing everyone except Grammie
plastic pens
that seem way too
flimsy for such a task.

We sign.
        And we hand back the contract.

'Fifty thousand dollars on the nose,' Caroline says,
'and how would you like that?
Cheque or bank transfer?'

Grammie almost spits out her dentures.

Dad's frown dissolves.
'Cheque,' he says.
'They'll take a cheque.'

Preamble

Caroline spends an eternity interviewing us
off camera:
      questions and questions and questions,
      all of which we've heard a thousand
      times before.

We could be rude,
      yawn or feign offence
      but the money hasn't cleared in our account
      yet.

The Crew

Caroline returns
with two men
in their twenties.
'This is Paul,' she says,
pointing at the guy in the baseball cap.
Turning to the other one
with a red beard, she says,
'And this is Shane.
We'll all be around for a while
so we better try to get
along.'

I wait a second for
Tippi to speak, but she doesn't.
'Of course,' I say.
'I'm sure we'll get along just fine.'

And when I look at Tippi
she is blushing
        deep puce.

'You like one of the camera guys,'
I say later
when we are alone.

'Don't be *absurd*,' she says,
far too passionately
for me to be wrong.

To Russia with Love

We pay for Dragon's dance trip to Russia
and
    she leaves on a bus stuffed full of other dancers
                for the airport.

We wave and blow kisses as
    she presses her fingertips against the window
                and then her lips.

She's taken
every tutu and
pair of ballet slippers she owns,
plus all our woolly hats and gloves
because we read about the
burly Russian cold,
where snow settles to the height
of mountains in places.

'Don't forget to come back,' Tippi told
her,
        zipping up the suitcase.

259

Dragon laughed
without looking at either of us,
because if she got the chance to stay in Russia
and dance forever
I'm sure
that's exactly what she would do.

And I wouldn't blame her.

Caroline Is Not Happy

'Your sister was meant to be in the documentary.
This wasn't part of our deal,'
Caroline says.

'So quit,' Tippi tells her,
'and we'll give you back the money.'

Tippi holds on to her poker face
like a top table player
in Las Vegas.

Caroline can't compete.
'Fine, but no more surprises.'

Whiskey Before Noon

When Dad gets home
he scuttles straight down the hallway
trying to avoid the cameras.
But Grammie's left her bowling bag in the way and
he ends up
      splattered across the floor like a
      joke.

Caroline laughs.
'Don't tell us you've been on the whiskey before
  noon,'
she says.

She sees his face
riddled with guilt
and must smell the alcohol.
'Oh,' she says. 'Oh, right.'
And her smile vanishes.

Behind the Bedroom Door

It takes five hours of
talking
shouting
and crying
behind
the bedroom door
for Mom and Dad
to come to an
agreement.

A Family Meeting

We gather at the kitchen table to hear the news:
Dad is moving out.

He can't stay sober
and Mom won't let the world
watch him drink.

'I'll be back when Caroline's finished,'
he says,
like this is the most sensible of solutions
and Caroline is the problem.

'How about you give up the booze?'
Tippi suggests.

Dad blinks and clings to a cushion.
We wait and watch
as his face
becomes an open
      plate
of despair.
'I can't,' he says.
      'I don't know how.'

We nod.
It's the most truthful thing
he's said in months.

Gone

Dad doesn't
dig out a bulky black suitcase from the cellar
like the one Dragon packed for Russia,
a suitcase with wheels and tags
and the promise of going
somewhere far away,

far better.

He manages to fit everything he's taking
into a red sports bag.

If you didn't know he was leaving
you'd think he was off to the gym
to pound away on a treadmill—
run for miles and miles
without getting anywhere
until finally coming home,
sweaty and smiling.

But Dad *is* going somewhere.

He is leaving us
        to live with his brother in New Brunswick.

Maybe I should be crying,
but as Dad closes the front door
behind him,
my tears don't come—
only a deep breath
and a very warm feeling of relief.

For the Best

'Your dad's gone, *too*?' Caroline asks.
She throws her hands into the air.
'Seriously?'

We shrug.

Paul and Shane blink.

Caroline
scratches her head.
Then she puts her hands into her pockets.

'Oh well.
It's probably for the best.'

Paul

Tippi drops her backpack
and Paul,
the cameraman,
picks it up for her.
She doesn't look at him
when she says,
'Thank you.'

Laughter

On Hudson Street
a toddler kicks his mom and runs off
at a sprint,
her chasing and screaming.
I'm not sure why, but it makes me laugh hard
and
it isn't long before Tippi is giggling, too.

Paul's camera is trained right at us,
sunbeams reflecting off the lens.

Caroline says,
'You laugh a lot. It's inspiring.
Even in your condition, you embrace life.'

But I'm not sure
what I'm supposed to do with life
other than embrace it.

Should I reject it?

I don't.
Instead I laugh.

And Caroline is inspired.

The Hiltons

We often get compared to Daisy and Violet Hilton,
'Because you're both so pretty,'
Caroline says,
and sighs.

But nothing good ever came of
Daisy and Violet's beauty
except for a few slimy suitors
sniffing around and hoping to bed them both
      —two for the price of one—
        let-me-get-a-look-at-you-with-no-panties-on
        kind of proposals.

They were born in 1908 and sold like slaves
to a midwife called Mary who
sent them touring across the world,
amazing the crowds with their singing
and saxophone playing
and being cheerful and charming
        despite their disability.

By our age Daisy and Violet were among
the wealthiest
performers of their time

and maybe we should learn from them,
be more brazen about selling our wares and
showcasing our abnormalities:

    'Step up, step up,
    see the two-headed girl
    play badminton!'

But like most conjoined twins in history,
the Hiltons' story ends in tragedy
when the public lost interest
and they were left broke,
spending seven long years
working behind a shop counter
and dying side by side
of Hong Kong flu.

They were found by a neighbour
and buried beneath a tombstone that reads
Beloved Siamese Twins
as though that was the
one and only thing
they were,
or that ever mattered
to anyone.

Popularity

Kids we hardly know,
kids who sidestepped us from day one,
start to sniff around
when they hear
we're about to shoot some scenes
for Caroline's film at school.
Permission slips are forged
and all the students in our class
offer themselves up
for interviews,
clamouring for a way in—
the chance to be a talking head
and show the world
how liberal and kindhearted they can be.

But Tippi and I have already told Caroline
who should be
getting airtime,
who deserves the limelight,
and it isn't anyone who has
spent the entire term
ignoring us.

Yasmeen and Jon
will be the stars.

Constantly Rolling

Caroline and the crew
follow us everywhere,
the camera
constantly rolling
so they won't
miss a thing.

I am used to being watched
and have sort of stopped noticing they are
there in the mornings
as I fumble around
getting ready,
as Tippi and I dry our hair, tie our shoes,
and snatch circles of buttered bagels for breakfast.

Sometimes we do something
completely ordinary,
like sweep the kitchen floor,
and Caroline lets her jaw drop
to show how fascinating
we are.

'Wow!' she'll say.
And then again,
'Wow.'

I just find it funny
that's she's paid us for this,
and that
something so boring
could ever
make it to TV.

A Postcard

I love it here.
All we do is DANCE!
Don't make me come back to New Jersey . . .
Love, Dragon
xxxxxxx

LATE
NOVEMBER

Snow

The brown, yellow, and red leaves of fall
have disintegrated to dust.

The white sky opens
and snow descends.

It is winter.

Collapse

Lumbering across the quadrangle on our way
to French,
it is
Tippi who collapses,
hitting the gravel
hard
and
    I spill right on top of her.

Caroline gasps
and Paul drops the camera,
which cracks against the ground.

I wait a few seconds.

I wait
for Tippi's eyes to open—
for her to shoo Caroline away with a casual
'I'm OK,
I'm OK.'

But those words do not come.

Caroline seizes my shirt.
'I can't find her pulse.
Why can't I feel her bloody heart beating?'
      and

'For Christ's sake, someone call an ambulance!'

Shane phones for help.

And help arrives.

We speed along the
highway
in the back of an ambulance,
wires plugged into us both
and beeping like an alarm
in the background.

My heart pounds
and I wait.

My breath thins
and I wait.

I wait
for Tippi's eyes to open.
But they do not.

Because this time

we are not
OK.

Hospital

The walls of the room are white and clean—
all signs of yesterday's sorrows scrubbed
away with bleach.

The lights are bright and above the quiet
bulky TV set in the corner
is a painting of a poppy field.

Perhaps it's meant to be soothing,
but for some reason
it makes me think
of war,
of teenagers running into a field at dawn
then falling down dead,
red blood blooming beneath their bodies.

Someone close by is sucking on a sweet,
the hard sound echoing in the small room
along with Tippi's quiet breathing.

I want to speak,
say that I am ready to get up and go home,
if she is.

But I am so tired
I cannot talk.

I close my eyes and
    darkness reclaims me.

In the Darkness

I wake again.
Tippi's eyes are wide and on me.
'What's happening to us?' I say.

'We'll figure it out,' she replies,
      and holds me.

Testing

Mom, Dad, and Grammie are dozing in
armchairs when an orderly strolls in,
his rubber shoes squeaking on the
linoleum.

'Let's go, girls!'
he says
in a thick Jersey accent
and whistles while he
wheels us down the corridor,
as if we are going for a couple of pedicures
and not being taken for testing,
where doctors will scan and probe and
devour our privacy.

I cross my fingers on both hands for luck,

like that could alter the outcome.

The Visitor

We've been
transferred to the Rhode Island Children's Hospital,
almost two hundred miles from home,
so Yasmeen and Jon
cannot come to visit.
Instead they text a million times a day
and send pictures
from The Church
of themselves drinking, smoking,
pretending to kill each another,
which make us laugh
and long to be better.

Our only visitor
apart from Mom, Dad, and Grammie
is Caroline Henley,
who comes every day
and secretly brings things no one else will
let us have,
like chips and soda.

Paul and Shane do not come with her
and she doesn't mention
the documentary
or all the money she's paid to peer at our lives.

I want to be suspicious,
but Caroline,
it seems,
cares.

Decency

'It doesn't make any sense,' Tippi says
when Caroline opens our window
to let out the smell of the morning's bacon.
'You paid a lot for full access and now,
when it gets exciting,
you don't even want an interview.
No one can be that noble.'

Caroline pulls a Kleenex from
her bag and blows her nose
hard.
'I'm not noble,' Caroline says.
'But I *am* a human being.'

'A very decent human being,' Tippi tells her,
and smiles.

Me

Mom is carrying an old Scrabble box
and a bag of clementines.
'Where's Dad?' I ask.

Mom points at the window.
'He's parking the car,' she says.
'Why? Did you think he might be at a bar?'

I shrug.

Mom sniffs.
'Good God, Gracie,
it really is time
you started focusing
on yourself.'

Results

Dr Derrick's office doors open
and we are pushed inside in an
    especially wide wheelchair.

I hold Tippi's hand tightly and wait for the verdict.

But Dr Derrick does not put it simply.

He displays scans and diagrams
and talks
    and talks
        and talks,
galloping through explanations of the
MRIs, echocardiograms,
gastrointestinal contrast studies,
and all the other big tests
we've been put through this week.

I stop listening to watch a bird on the tree outside
hop along a branch and
peep
in the window at us
like a regular paparazzo.

Finally Dad raises a hand,
stops Dr Derrick dead,
and says, 'And what does this all *mean*
for my daughters?'

Dr Derrick taps his forefingers together in time
to the wall clock ticking above him and says,
'The prognosis together is not good.'

We are silent.
He continues.

'Grace has developed cardiomyopathy
and Tippi is supporting her,
supporting her and a very dilated heart.
We can't repair the damage.
The only course of action
in the long term
is to replace the whole heart.
If we don't,
Grace will get sicker,
they both will,
until . . .'

He looks at a graph like the terrible answers
are buried in its lines.

'I have to recommend a separation.
We would keep Grace stable with drugs and
a ventricular device until she'd recovered.
Then she would go on a transplant list.'

I do not know how to hold
everything Dr Derrick is saying in my head
all at once.

It is so much.
It is too much.
It is more than I could have imagined.
And it is all my fault.
All my stupid heart's fault.

'Separation at this age is tricky and very unusual,'
Dr Derrick goes on.
'It isn't without massive risks and costs,
especially to Grace,
but it looks like the only option
we've got
left.'

He pushes papers at us—

step by step instructions on how to
carve

    a space
    between
    two people
    before ripping

         out the heart of one of them.

My insides harden.
My blood pumps fast.
My head spins.

'No. Absolutely not.
We'll take our chances as we are,' Tippi says.
'You can knock us both out
and put a new heart in.
Or do whatever it is you have to do.
You don't have to separate us first.
Don't say you have to do that.'

Dr Derrick makes his face a rock.
'Grace isn't eligible for a transplant while conjoined.
We can't do anything to help her
if she's still attached to you.
The drugs alone
would put you in too much danger.'

He pauses to give us time to
think about what this means,
to contemplate our own demise,
and taps his forefingers together again.

We all stare speechless at Dr Derrick, who might as
  well be God.

I let go of Tippi's hand
and pull myself up straight
because Dr Derrick is right,
I am the problem,
me and my dying heart,
and his solution is fitting.

'We should give it a go,' I say.
And for both of us: 'Yes, let's do it.'

Mom goes white.
'Might be best to think about it overnight,' she says.

'Or longer,' Dad adds.
'I mean, what's changed?
How can it have changed?'

Dr Derrick blinks.
'When I saw you last time
you were fine.
Nothing too worrying at all.
But.
I suspect . . .
I suspect it was the flu that did it.
A viral infection is often to blame for
cardiomyopathy.
It's just terrible luck that Grace's heart reacted as it
  did.'

Silence seeps into the room again.
The bird outside
      flies away with wide wings.

And then Mom speaks. She wants the statistics.
She wants Dr Derrick to tell her
in hard, whole numbers what the chances are
of any number of tragedies
befalling us.

'I believe there is a possibility we can be successful,'
is all he can say.

And I know what this means.

I have read reports.

I have read old newspapers.

When conjoined twins are separated,
it's deemed a success so
long as one of them lives.

For a while.

And that,
to me,
is the saddest thing
I know about how
people see us.

'Give me numbers,' Mom insists.
'I want to know what happens if we do nothing.'

Dr Derrick sighs.
He closes the files on his desk
and leans forward.
'Left as it is,
they'll both die.'

Mom starts to cry.
Dad holds her hand.

'With a separation, they have hope,
a fighting chance,
but I can't put a number on it.
If I did, it would be low.
It would be quite low.'

Mom whimpers
and then Dad does, too.

'I know this isn't good news.
But go home.
Take time to think it over.
Until then, no school. Nothing strenuous.
Eat and sleep properly.
And keep away from cigarettes and alcohol,'
  Dr Derrick says.

He smiles suddenly making it sound like we
have a choice
and years to figure this out,
when I know,
deep down,
we don't.

Time is already
running out.

Gratis

Before we leave Rhode Island,
        our dirty clothes
        balled up in clear plastic bags,
Dr Derrick
        pops his head into our room and asks to
speak to Mom and Dad again
        privately.

They leave looking ashen
        but return with their faces
        halved of worry.

'The entire team will do the procedures for free,'
Mom tells us,
'if that's what you decide you want.'

Tippi and I have cost our family
a fortune,
yet the most expensive procedure of all
        they will do for nothing.

They needn't
pretend this is a kindness:

everyone knows that
no matter what happens to us,
an operation like that would make the doctors
  famous,
and that's worth a lot more to them
          than dollars in the bank.

An Elephant in the Room

On the drive home, Dad tells terrible jokes
that we've heard before
but which we laugh at anyway,
loudly,
fearful of what we'd have to discuss if he
stopped.

It's as though we are a carefree, unbroken family,
like the ones you see in advertisements for laundry
  detergent.
It's as though we haven't been in the hospital,
as though we're returning from a trip to the beach
and wearing good moods like glimmering tans.

It's as though we haven't understood that if we go
  ahead
we'll both be left with one leg and hip and be
  wheelchair bound
for life.
It's as though no one knows
I'm quietly killing Tippi.

Mom points to a McDonald's. 'Lunch?'

Usually I would complain about animal welfare,
about cows kept in fields full of their own shit,
but today I am shamed and silent as
Tippi licks her lips and lists all the
McFlurry flavors.

We pull into the drive-thru
and eat smelly burgers
and thick shakes from our laps,
the traffic blaring by
so we can't hear each other chew or swallow
or breathe.

And even when we get home and Dad makes coffee
(like he still lives here),
we pretend everything is perfect
and that the elephant in the room who is heaving
  down our necks
is nothing but a mouse, way more scared of us
than we are of it.

A Heart That Beats for Two

If I were a singleton
I might have dropped dead by now.

Instead
my sister bears the burden of keeping me alive,
of pumping most of the blood around our bodies.

Instead
I freeload.

And she
doesn't complain.

A Parasite

She makes me look at her,
holding my chin with cold fingertips.
'We're doing fine as we are,' she says.
She says, 'We're meant to be together.
If we separate, we'll die.'

Tippi's lips are dry.
Her face is grey.
She looks likes she's
lived longer than
anyone I know.

'You think we're partners but really
        I'm a parasite,' I whisper.
'I don't want to suck
        your life from you.'

'Oh come on, Grace,' she says,
'all this *you* and *me* is a lie.
There has only ever been *us*.
So
I won't do it.
You can't *make* me
have an operation.'

'But I'm a parasite,' I repeat,
and in my head say it
over and over.
Parasite. Parasite. Parasite.
All I want now is to save Tippi.

If I can.

DECEMBER

Welcome

Caroline Henley is back.
'Do you mind?
I know it's a difficult time,'
she says.

Despite her contract,
she hasn't tried to film anything
or get an interview
in over two weeks.

She has proven she isn't the paparazzi.
She has proven she won't take
our lives and turn them
into a sensational story
but hold them gently
and mould her movie
around the
truth.

And so Caroline is welcome—
welcome to film us,
                    our decision,
and what
might be
the last few months of
our lives.

The Things I Tell Dr Murphy

'You know,
I've spent so
long trying to convince everyone
that I'm an individual,
that Tippi's my twin
but not me,
that I've never really thought about
how it would be if
we weren't together,
how
losing her would be like
lying in a pyre
and waiting for the flames.

She's not a piece of me.

She's me entirely
and without her
there would be
a gaping space
in my chest,
an expanding black hole
that nothing
else could
fill.

You know?

Nothing else could fill that space.'

Dr Murphy sits back in her chair.
        'Finally you're opening up,'
        she says.

        Right.
        All these years
        she hadn't been
buying my bullshit at all.

Catching Up

Although it's a Saturday
and Hornbeacon is closed up,
and although Mom is terrified of us leaving her
  sight,
Grammie drives us to Montclair where
Yasmeen and Jon meet us on the school's front steps.

Yasmeen is clutching a pile of papers,
wearing a frown,
and glowering at us.
Her hair is no longer hot pink
but dark denim blue,
her bangs tickling her eyes.

Jon stands behind her
blinking against the sun,
a silver gum wrapper stuck to his sneaker.

Carefully they reach for us then hold on tight.

'You losers have a lot to do,' Yasmeen says.
'I'm not sure how you'll catch up before the
  semester ends.'

She slams a heavy wad of papers
against Tippi's chest.

'We won't be back for a while.
You think we're going to spend our dying days
working on the French conditional?' Tippi asks,
pitching the multicoloured papers into the air so
   they
scatter like supersized confetti
across the courtyard.

'You're so dramatic,' Yasmeen says,
and rolls her half-hidden eyes.
'So what are you guys doing instead?
Do you even have a bucket list?'

Behind us Caroline clears her throat.
'We're filming,' she warns.

'Who cares?' Tippi asks,
and we hobble off to The Church.

Bucket Lists

Sitting on a log,
Tippi and I write up our lists,
shoulders curled away from each other,
hands hiding our words.
But I can't think of much:
> 1) *Read* Jane Eyre
> 2) *Watch the sun rise*
> 3) *Climb a tree*
> 4) *Kiss a boy—for real*

Tippi looks over my shoulder.
'I've heard *Jane Eyre*'s a real bore,'
she says,
then hands me her list.
This is what she has written:
> 1) *Stop being such a bitch*

'That's gonna take some time,'
I tell her.

'And so is your number four,' she says.

Easy

Yasmeen runs a jagged nail down my list.
'Ugh,' she says.
'Couldn't you have added something
cool like
running naked through the school hallways
or getting whipped by pint-sized circus clowns?'

'She's done both those things already,'
Tippi says,
and I laugh very, very loudly,
hoping Jon won't look at my list
and hoping he will.

'You've never climbed a tree?'
Yasmeen asks,
then quickly says,
'Jon, you gotta kiss Grace.'
She slams my list into his hand
like a court summons.
'And lend her this stupid book.'

'He doesn't have to do anything,' I mumble.

Jon runs his eyes over the paper
and puts out his cigarette.
He bites his bottom lip.
'I've an old copy of *Jane Eyre* you can keep.
I'll drive it over to your place,' he says.

'Oh, for the love of God, a kiss is just a kiss,'
   Yasmeen says.

But she is wrong:
a kiss from Jon
would mean

Everything.

Nightmare

In the public library next to Church Square Park
where Tippi and I go to borrow free movies,
a girl with an iPhone
huffs and sighs.
'My phone's lost its signal. I can't connect to the
  Wi-Fi.
What a *nightmare*,'
she tells her friend,
waving the phone around
and hoping to catch a stray ray
of connectivity in the air.

Isn't it funny what people worry about
when their lives are going
swimmingly?

I Slip Away

Shane has the flu
and won't risk coming anywhere near us,
so when Caroline's busy
taking calls
or arranging interviews,
Paul's the only one
following us around.

When I can,
I become invisible.

I put in my headphones
and
        slip away.

I try
as hard as I can
to give Tippi
a little
time with
him.

'I know what you're doing,'
she says.

'But it's not like you and Jon.
It's nothing.'

'But it could be something,'
I say.

'Look at me, Grace,' Tippi replies.
'Do you think he'd ever
be interested in a
brunette?'

She laughs.
And so do I.

A Replacement

Aunty Anne brings Beau, our newest cousin,
to visit.
He is all drool and whimpers
yet we fight over who gets to hold him,
who changes his diaper and
gives him his bottle.

Aunty Anne yawns and says,
'Everyone keeps asking when I'll have the next one.
But I'm so tired.'

Mom titters and gives her sister a mild backrub.
'It gets easier. They sleep through the night soon
   enough.'

Aunty Anne closes her eyes.
'My friend told me to have another child
in case anything ever happened to Beau.
I hate even having to imagine it.'

Mom's hands freeze.
Baby Beau mewls, sensing our attention is
elsewhere.
'The pain of losing one child
wouldn't vanish just because you have another,'
  Mom says.

'You can't make replacements.'

Film

Caroline leaves the cameras in our bedroom
every night
so she doesn't have to haul them
back and forth from New York City
every day.
They sit on our desk and we don't pay them any
attention
at all
until
I remember that the crew has been filming
everyone.

I slide a tiny green button sideways
and watch.
We watch.
And we see
Mom and Dad's crinkled faces
as Caroline softly asks,
'Do you think Tippi and Grace
should be separated?'

Dad stares into his lap.

'I want to keep them alive,' Mom says.
'No parent should bury a child,
and definitely not two of them.
But it's up to them to decide.
It's up to them.'

We watch
Mom cry into the camera
and beg Caroline to turn it off,
and then we stare at each other
thinking exactly the same thing.

This isn't just about us.

No Run-throughs

In English class we were encouraged to write
drafts and make edits
until our words were as clear
as filtered water.
In math we were warned to
review our workings,
ensure the figure at the end
was correct.
And in music we rehearsed
songs a hundred times,
trying out a glut of harmonies
before Mr Hunt was satisfied.

Yet when it matters,
when it's a life-and-death decision,
like whether to slice ourselves
                              apart or not,
we've no way to perfect the path we're taking
and have only
one choice
        and
one chance
        to get it right.

Obviously

We meet Dr Derrick to give him our decision
and he is silent for several moments,
his face stone,
none of the excitement we expected seeping
  through,
no relishing the risks involved,
and I wonder whether we've underestimated him.
'I'll get the planning under way,' he says,
'This is a big project and it won't happen
overnight.
But we can't wait too long, either.'
He looks at me directly.
'Obviously, we can't wait too long.'

The Call

Yasmeen calls us after midnight.
'You can relax.
Jon and I have figured it all out.
Winter break we're going on a road trip.
My uncle has a place in Montauk.
It's going to be awesome.'

Tippi and I grin.

'We're in,' we say together.

Whether Mom Likes It or Not

Mom is absolutely
one hundred percent
against letting us go anywhere near

                           Long Island.
'You think I'm going to let you roam around the
   country
with your hearts about to screech to a stop at any
   moment,
and without a drop of adult supervision?
Do you know me at all?
Do you?'
Mom asks.
She nips her lips shut.

But Tippi's lips are even thinner.
'I know you're worried. We're sorry about that.
But this isn't a negotiation.
We're going whether you like it or not,' Tippi says.
'We're going to Long Island with our friends
and there's not a shit-flicking thing anyone can say
   to stop us.'

Road Trip

Mom keeps checking the internet,
refreshing the pages
    over and over
    for news of
    bad weather or
    traffic accidents on Long Island,
anything that might
prevent us from going.
She pokes around in her purse every few minutes
 and pulls out things
like Kleenex and cough candies
that 'might come in handy on the trip.'
She paces the floor.
She checks her watch.
She refreshes the internet again.

Dad is visiting for the weekend.
He is making risotto,
guarding the pot and incessantly stirring.
'Try to stop worrying,' he tells Mom,
and behind his back she rolls her eyes
as if to say,
      What would you know?

Apparently he hasn't taken a drink in ten days,
says he's been going to recovery meetings,
and while Tippi and I don't hold our breaths,
we see how Mom is revelling a little in his normality,
grinning at jokes and delighting in his overcooked
    dinners.

'I actually think it's very unfair to keep Caroline
    from going, too,'
Mom says.
'A deal's a deal.
What kind of film will it be without footage of the
    trip?'

Caroline is leafing through an old photo album,
picking out the pictures to take away and scan.
'It works for me actually,' she says.
'Paul's taking a few days off
to see his brother in Boston,
and poor Shane's still sick with
the flu.'

'Cool,'
I say
trying not to feel resentful
of Shane

or the millions of other people
whose hearts don't die
because they get a little virus.

A car horn honks
and Dad drags our bag out to the curb where Jon
throws it into the trunk of the car.
We strap ourselves into the back seat
and wave to Mom who has taken
our places by the bay window,
where I'm sure she'll stand until we return.

Dad goes back inside.
Jon jumps into the driver's seat and looks at us in
the rearview mirror. 'Did you bring booze?' he
  asks.

I delve into our duffle bag and Jon leans over the
  seat to
look at the bounty of beers and wine and vodka
we've pinched from Dad's dormant stash
in the kitchen.

'You're the best,' he says. 'Now let's get out of here.'

Pit Stop

We've only driven for an hour when Yasmeen
announces she's hungry,
that she wants Burger King
or something equally disgusting
to help her stay awake while we drive the measly
   three hours east.
Jon pulls over at a service station
and Yasmeen jumps out.

Jon turns up the radio and grabs a beer bottle
from our bag,
         twisting it open.
'Aren't you coming?' Yasmeen asks.
'Couldn't you just murder a burger?'

Tippi opens her door and starts to pull on me.

But I don't want to go anywhere.
I want to sit in the car with Jon,
sharing a beer I shouldn't be drinking
and listening to the radio.

'Come on,' Tippi says. 'Burgers.'

I hold my body rigid.

'What's wrong with you?' Tippi asks.

'Nothing,' I say.

'So come on,' she repeats.
'You too, Jon.'

He shakes his head.
'I'm good with beer and rock music.
Be sure to pick up some Cokes for the vodka
after you've eaten your delicious
Brazilian rainforest beef.'

Yasmeen gives him the finger
and takes Tippi's hand.
'Don't drink more than one of those,' she
  tells Jon,
and suddenly my body is
out of the car and in the lot,
waiting for a table,
eating fries,
and paying the check.

I go through all the motions of
being in the restaurant
with Tippi and Yasmeen
while all the time
my mind is on Jon—
the back of his head,
the lines of his neck,
his smell,
his voice.

His everything.

The Barn

The library is piled high with old copies of art
   magazines
and books so yellowed and dry they look like they'd
crack down the middle if you tried to read them.
The bathroom has no light and mould creeps from
   the corners
of the shower and across the walls.
The kitchen is dappled in tiny brown mouse
   droppings
and dead beetles.

Upstairs
        Yasmeen and Jon
        rearrange the furniture,
        drag a double bed with
a sunken mattress into the biggest of the rooms so
   that
two beds
are pushed up together
against the wall making a massive one
        for four.
The cobwebby window is wiped clean with the cuff
of Yasmeen's coat.
Jon sweeps the floor.

I plug in a heater and we all stand around it,
red–nosed,
hands in our armpits.

This is not like the other holiday homes
we saw as we drove through the Hamptons,
milk-white mansions with colonnades and crystal
  blue fountains,
but it is ours and no one else's for three days,
so the bugs, peeling paint, and
rusting pipes don't really worry me very much at
all.

In Bed

Tippi gets Yasmeen's shoulder to lean on.
I lie next to Jon.

By candlelight he reads aloud from *Ulysses*,
words with a melody,
some unrecognisable gems glittering
in the gloom.
'Pain, that was not yet the pain of love,
fretted his heart,' he reads,
then seeing that both Tippi's and Yasmeen's eyes are
   shut,
stops and closes the book.

I rest a hand on his hand.
Hold his eyes with my eyes.
'Please keep reading,' I beg,
        and he does.

Long into the night
it is the two of us alone
with Joyce's voice between us.
'You read beautifully,' I tell him.

'And tomorrow night it's your turn,'
he says.

The book is closed with a gentle huff.
The candle is blown out.
Jon curls his body around mine
so that his breath is on my cheek.

'Good night,' he whispers
and within minutes is asleep
beside me.

To the Lighthouse

Salty eyed and stiff from the cold,
we wake in the dark and
tiptoe downstairs in our socks
to cook up a
tower of pancakes
which we eat with
so much syrup
my teeth ache.

Fishermen in waders stand on rocks,
the Atlantic Ocean enveloping them—
sloshing at their edges like
angry, fizzing soda.
And as they leave,
carrying buckets full of edible sea monsters,
a light beam punctures the morning.

The sky blushes, letting go of its darkness.
The fringe of the horizon is pink.

'Sunrise,' Tippi says.
'It makes me want to believe in God.'

'Me, too,' Yasmeen tells her.

And no one else says another word
until the sun is an orange orb
and our asses are numb
from sitting so long.

Skinny-dipping

Skinny-dipping isn't on either of our bucket lists
but Yasmeen says it's on hers,
so that's what we're doing.
Not in the bitter sea
where the surf is high and threatens to
kidnap anyone silly enough to plunge into her,
but in a neighbour's pool.
'It can be heated, so she keeps the water
in it even in the winter,'
Yasmeen tells us.
'But she's only here on weekends.
We have all day.'

We sneak up the side of the cedar-panelled house
and unroll the pool's plastic covering.
Leaves float on the water
like herbs in a clear soup.
Even before Jon has used a net to clear the leaves,
Yasmeen is in her purple bra and pink panties,
toes testing the water.
And then her underwear is off
and she
     dives
        like an eagle

into the deep end and comes up screeching
and blue.

Jon is next to take off his shirt and pants.
I look away
and only turn around when I hear his body
dive-bombing the water
and the profanities tumbling out of him
like urgent prayers.

'What do you think?' I ask Tippi.
No one except our parents and the doctors have
   seen
us undressed before,
and I am terrified of
how I must look to others,
of how disgusted
a person
would be
if he saw us
stripped bare.

'What's the worst that could happen?' I ask
thinking suddenly of our health,
                    of our hearts.

Then I throw off my coat.

Naked
we plunge feet first into the pool
and flail when the frost, like needles, meets our
  skin.

Jon cheers and swims closer.
'Refreshing, huh?' he says.

And just as we are about to get out,
Yasmeen shouts and points to the house,
where a face is plastered against the window,
the mouth a perfect zero.

'Let's *go*!' Yasmeen yells.

Clumsily we climb from the pool,
grabbing our clothes and covering ourselves
with our coats as best we can
before plodding across the lawn
and
down the street to home.

'Her expression was priceless!' Yasmeen squeals,
pushing open the barn door.

A mouse scurries under the oven
and no one suggests we set a trap to kill it.
We just open the refrigerator door
and take out four bottles of beer.

No More

Mom sends a text.
Are you having fun?

She sends another.
Are you alive?

And another.
I'm worried.

And finally.
I'm going to call the cops.

So I text her back and warn her not to
send any more messages.

Number Four

Jon and I are the last ones awake again.

After we've read for an hour,
he stares up at the ceiling and says,
'I feel bad about what happened
when you showed me the bucket list.'

I pretend I don't know what he means.
'I finished *Jane Eyre*.
And I love Mr Rochester.
I think that's what Tippi and I need.
Blind men who've lost everything.'

I try to laugh but
nothing comes out.

Jon sits up
and lights a cigarette.

'Grace . . .
        . . . the thing is . . .'

I stop him.

'I get it.
I really get it.
I know how I look
and what that means for my life.'

I touch the place where Tippi and I are joined,
where the doctors plan to place tissue expanders
that will make our bodies look
like we are covered in molehills.

'I can't explain what I feel,' he says.
'I read all these books,
so many words,
but I don't own any.
I don't know what's happening
inside me.
I can't get it out.'

He crushes the cigarette into a dirty plate,
puts a piece of gum into his mouth, and
shuts off the light.

He slides down next to me
and rests his forehead against mine.

'Oh, Grace,' he says,
and cups my face in his hands.

'Jon,' I whisper,
and
then
his mouth is on mine,
his tongue that tastes of watermelon gum
prying my lips open
and we are kissing—breath heavy,
and kissing—heart light,
and kissing and kissing
and all I can I do when he stops
is inhale deeply
and say,
'I don't know what's happening inside me, either.'

Watermelon

I wake up still tasting the watermelon
from his mouth.

After I've brushed my teeth the flavour fades so
I ask Jon for a piece of gum
and spend all day
with the taste
of his kiss
in my mouth.

Weirdo

'He kissed me last night,' I whisper to Tippi
when we are alone.

She looks at me sideways
as though I've offered her a rotten tuna sandwich.
'If Jon's seriously interested in you,
he's a weirdo.
You get that, right?'

I look down at our shared legs.
'I thought you were trying to be
less of bitch,' I say.

She grins.
'This is me trying.'

Planning

Yasmeen licks the tip of her pencil, finds a
clean page
in her notebook,
and waits for Tippi and me to outline our funeral
directions,
individual plans and a joint one, too,

                              just in case.

Jon has gone to the store for snacks.
He doesn't want to hear any of this.
Says he can't.

Yasmeen's the only person who will
listen
and promise to carry out our wishes
without accusing us of being
morbid
or crying her eyes out at the thought of us leaving.
She's the only person, like us, who's
been coping with dying since she was born.
It doesn't freak her out.
Not too much
        anyway.

'Music?' Yasmeen asks, and without skipping a beat
Tippi tells her,
'A lot of Dolly Parton for me.
"I Will Always Love You"
is a good one.
I like "Home", too.'

'Look, I love Dolly as much as the next person,
but you really want *her* at your funeral?'
Yasmeen asks.
She uses her hands to outline Dolly's
curves in the air.

'If people are thinking about Dolly's tits,
they won't be
thinking about mine,' Tippi says.

'And no hymns,' I add. 'I don't want anything holy.
God is not invited to our funeral.'

Yasmeen nods and makes a note on the paper.
'So something satanic? Not. A. Problem.'

We stuff cashews into our mouths
and Yasmeen goes on cheerfully.
'Coffins. Joint or separate?'

'Joint,' we say together without having to confer
because what else could make sense?

'Unless one of us lives, in which case,
separate would be the way to go,' Tippi says,
and laughs though with very little verve.

And we continue.

We fully plan the services and burials,
and when we're done
Yasmeen scrolls through her phone until she finds a
   Dolly Parton track,
and we all sing
as Yasmeen dances
around the kitchen,
repeating the refrain from 'Jolene' again and again,
like it's the most cheerful song in the world.

The Promise

Despite Dr Derrick's warnings,
we sit on the beach at night
smoking cigars and drinking
miniature bottles of gin,
a fire pit blazing
in the sand.

'I'm drunk,' Tippi says,
falling backwards,
taking me with her.

We stare at the sickle moon,
our heads spinning,
and without thinking much about it
I say, 'Do you promise to live
without me, if I don't make it?'

The sea stops roaring.
The fire puts a finger to its fizzing lips.

'I promise to marry Jon,' Tippi says,
giggling,
tickling my side with her fingers.

'Seriously,' I say.

Tippi pulls me to sitting and takes another slug of
 gin.
'I promise, if you do.'

'I do,' I say,
and kiss her.

Last Night

'I have a confession,' Jon says
to the darkness.

I make my hands into fists
and ready myself for the worst.

'I have no idea what James Joyce
is rambling on about,' he admits.

I uncurl.

'Me neither,' I say.
'But I love it anyway.'

'Yes,' he says.
'Isn't it funny how something
so abstract can still speak to us?'

He takes my hand and does not let go
until morning.

The Return

Pointe shoes hang from their ribbons on the
  coatrack.
Thick leg warmers are balled up by the radiator.
'Anyone home?' I call out.
'Dragon?'

She skips from the bathroom
and throws two slim arms around us.
'I *missed* you,' she says.
'I bought you Russian nesting dolls. They were
  cheap.
And I got a new boyfriend. His name is Peter.
He's a Muscovite.'

'I'm so sorry we dragged you back,'
I say.

Dragon shakes her head.
'Russia's freezing and Peter wanted to get into my
  panties.
Better to come home.
Besides, it isn't every day your
conjoined sisters separate.
I wanted to be here when . . .'

She runs away and comes back with the nesting
   dolls.

I pull the first doll apart and then the second.
Layer on layer she is the same:
a perfect circular red blush, little coal eyes,
and delving into
smaller versions
        reveals no more.

'You're looking for the symbolism, aren't you?'
Dragon says.
She grabs the dolls and
stuffs them back into each other.
'They're about motherhood.
They aren't about *you*.'

Tippi snickers.
'And there was Grace thinking that
        everything was about us.'

Christmas

We hang lights on the apple tree in our yard.
We eat too much turkey and stuffing.
We buy gifts.

It is Christmas
after all,
and at the end of the day
we're no
different
from any other family.

New Skin

Dr Derrick introduces someone new:
Dr Forrester, an expert in his field.
He is the one who slides skin expanders
—small balloons filled with saline—
under our skin to stretch it out
so we will have enough to cover the
wounds of separation
when the time comes.

We are awake for the procedure,
under a local anesthetic,
blinking against bright lights and
watching the nurses and doctors
hovering above us,
noses and mouths hidden behind green surgical
   masks.

Hours later
Tippi groans and I clutch the bedsheets
to stop myself from screaming out.
'We need Vicodin,' Tippi mutters,
pressing the call bell.

My body throbs and burns.

And these skin expanders are just the start.

'Soon it's going to look like you're covered in
colossal tumours,'
Dr Forrester tells us the next morning,
the corners of his mouth crusted in dried white
  spittle.
'But it will only be for a short time.
And you can go home while they work their magic.'

Without asking our permission, he presses his hands
  against
the incisions
—our bellies, backs, and sides—
and it is plain to me
that we no longer
own our bodies:
we have entrusted them to these men and women
who will inflate us and
shape us and
slice us apart
and never stop to ask,
Are you sure?

Jon

I know
he   doesn't mean to shudder as
he   touches the bump on
my   side where the tissue expanders are growing.

But
he   *does* shudder,
he   can't help it, and for the first time I realise that
he   is not perfect.

And
I   hate him for it.

JANUARY

A Waste

We wait for our skin to grow
and the doctors to be ready.
All we can really do
is wait
and read
and watch TV
and comply
with the nurse
who visits every day
to check we aren't overdoing it.

And I get to thinking
that all this waiting,
just waiting,
is a great big waste of
the last moments
of our lives.

Folding

One way or the other,
we soon won't
need the dresser full of
extra-wide pants and skirts,
not to mention the supersized panties
we've worn since we were potty trained.

So although we still ache a bit
from the skin expanders,
we spend some time
clearing our closets
of anything we won't be able to wear
once we are two,
holding up bright orange sweatpants
and wondering why we ever bought
them in the first place.

'We should go shopping,' I say.
Tippi turns
        the sterling silver ring on her
right index finger
        around and around.
'No,' she says. 'We should wait.
We should wait
and see what happens.'

Many

I rearrange the Russian nesting dolls,
sitting them
side by side
but
     all out of order,
taking them apart
     and putting them back together again,
          hiding one inside the other.
And it doesn't matter what Dragon says,
that they aren't about Tippi and me;
every time I hold the tenth one,
the tiniest that lives at the centre of them all,
as small and forgettable as a grain of rice,
I find myself wanting to
     throw her out with the garbage
     to see how
     the rest of the dolls
     get along
     without her.

How do you like that for symbolism?

The World Has Heard

Eventually
we are admitted to the hospital
so they can monitor our health
and
somehow the world quickly learns
we are here
and what
we plan to do.
The media
camps out
opposite Accident and Emergency
through snow and sleet
like frenzied teenage boy-band fans waiting for
   concert tickets
or a glimpse of their idols.

Tippi and I watch the crowd swell
            from five floors up,
but the only person we talk to is Caroline,
not that she follows us much any more,
preferring to interview the doctors
or our parents
and leaving us pretty much alone
to watch daytime TV and order low-fat yoghurt
from the hospital cafeteria.

At Dr Derrick's Request

Dr Murphy comes to see me in Rhode Island.
She is wearing a navy trouser suit
and thick-rimmed glasses,
looking so serious and severe
I know that Dr Derrick must have
told her
we haven't much hope
of surviving.

'So . . .' she says,
crossing her legs
and folding her hands in her lap.

We watch each other.

The big hand on the clock moves quickly.

'She'll be OK without me,' I lie.

Dr Murphy nods.
'And how would you be without her?'

'I'd be nothing,' I say.
'I'd disappear.
But that's not how this is going to happen.'

'Probably not.
But let's try to prepare you for whatever happens.'

I want to use my nails to score deep
red lines down Dr Murphy's face.
I want to ram my fist into her gut
and make her scream.
I want to tell her *Fuck the hell off*
and *Leave me alone,*
and *Stop making me imagine the future.*

I don't.
I lower my head.
Speak into my lap.
'I'm terrified.'

For the first time ever,
Dr Murphy leans forward
and takes one of my hands.
Even Tippi looks up.

'I'm terrified, too,'
Dr Murphy says.

The Power of Perception

Dr Forrester checks our skin where his
tissue expanders
have swollen up our sides.
'Looking beautiful, girls,' he says,
fingering the bulges.
What others have shuddered to see
makes Dr Forrester grin,
which says
quite a lot
about the
power of perception.

Mechanics

Dr Derrick explains the procedure a dozen times
with dolls and diagrams.
The separation alone will take over eighteen hours
and then I'll have Heartware fitted
and drugs injected to keep
me alive.
They'll induce comas in both of us for at least a
week
to save us from the
pain of recovery.

If I wake up . . .
If I survive . . .
I'll go on a list.

I'll go on a transplant list for a heart and wait
like a bloodthirsty vulture for
tragedy to befall another family.

The more he explains,
the more it sounds like magic.

I mean,
how can they reconstruct our lower halves

so that we end up with two whole bodies?
We share most of our
intestines
but Dr Derrick says this is not a problem.
We share our privates
but Dr Derrick says he'll give those pieces
to Tippi and
fix me up
so I'll be like any other girl when he's finished.

But this is a lie.

In any case, I don't question him
and I never
ask why he's decided to give the originals to Tippi
because it's a cold
hard
fact
that out of the two of us,
my chances of making it
out of the operating room alive
are
very,
very
slim.

Death

What does death feel like?
Sleeping?
Being in a dark and silent dream?

Maybe that would be OK—
if nothingness
is all it is.

But I'm kidding myself.

It must be worse than that or people
wouldn't so
furiously
avoid it.

Maybe death is white and

glaring.

Maybe it is a lack of sleep,

a pure awakening—

a deafening reality

that is truly
unbearable.

But no one will ever know
how it feels
until he arrives there.

All I know now is that it
looks like
a brass-handled coffin being
lowered
into the ground,

and
I've absolutely no interest
in
getting into one
of those things.

Experimental

Jon visits us in the hospital
without Yasmeen.
He puts a bunch of withering white roses
next to the bed
then gets busy finding a vase
and water and dribbles of soda
to bring the flowers back to life.
'Did you and Yasmeen argue?' Tippi asks.

'Me and Yasmeen? No. She's at a wedding,' he
  explains.
'And I didn't want to wait.
I wanted to see you.'

He stays several hours and as he leaves
he hugs us both
then kisses me quickly
—not with his whole
        watermelon mouth—
just the lips,
pressed almost chastely
against mine.

When he is gone Tippi asks,
'What does it mean? Are you guys an item?'

I shrug.
'I don't think so.'

'Maybe you're an experiment,' she says.
'But then again, what relationship isn't.'

'Was that a nice thing you just tried to say?' I ask,
nudging her.

She grins. 'Go to hell!'

Dreaming

Of him.
Dreaming of us,
bound together chest to chest,
hearts one.

But where has Tippi gone?

I cannot see her
            when I search
nor hear her when I
                        call out.

He says,
        'You've got me,'

but when I wake up

screaming

sweating

crying

I know that
he

is not
enough.

Climbing

Our family throws us a 'good luck' party
and we all pretend it's not a party to say
goodbye.

Everyone comes.

Cousins we haven't seen since their voices broke,
doctors we've known our whole lives,
and even Mrs James from Hornbeacon High, who
warns us we won't be given
special treatment when we return to school.
'You'll be expected to pass your finals
like everyone else,' she says.
She's trying to be kind but it's
a stupid thing to say;
if we live
we won't be able to walk
and special treatment will
be exactly what we need.

Yasmeen and Jon turn up the music so loud
a nurse holding a thermometer comes in to tell
us to keep it quiet because we are disturbing the
  other patients.

As everyone leaves,
Yasmeen pats our sides
like she's checking our pockets for change.
'See you soon, assholes,' she says,
and is gone,
unable to say any more.
Jon puts his arms around us both and
rests his head on my shoulder.
'It's always been complicated, you know.'
I allow my faltering heart some last thumps for him
before
I pull away.
        'Not today,' I say.

Caroline makes Paul take a picture
of us,
her face wedged between ours,
chocolate cake on her chin.
She says 'cheese' for about three seconds then
uses the photograph as her phone's home screen.
'I'll be in soon for follow-up interviews, OK?'
she says.
She squeezes our knees.
'You're both lovely.'

The music is switched off.

The food is cleared away.

Grammie turns on the TV
and Mom and Dad go to a room to sign more
    papers.
'I didn't complete my bucket list,' I say aloud
and Dragon pulls her chair closer.
'A bucket list?' she asks.

I gulp. 'A list of things to do before you die,' I
    explain.

Dragon flinches and her eyes grow wide
as she tries to hold in the tears.

'Grace never climbed a tree,' Tippi tells her.

'Well, let's go and do it,' Dragon says.
She hands us our crutches.

A nurse stops us by the elevator.
'Is there a problem?' she asks,
taking me by the elbow.

'We need some air,' I say.

The nurse shakes her head.
'No. No, I don't think that's a good idea.'

'But she's going to be sick,' Tippi says.
'At least get her a wheelchair.'

The nurse looks up and down the empty hallway.

'Fine.
Stay there.
Let me get one
and I'll come with you.'

'OK,' Tippi says,
and once the nurse is out of sight
we slip into the waiting elevator
and go
down
to the ground floor
and into the parking lot
to
scout for trees.

'There!' Dragon says,
pointing across the parkway at an oak,
its limbs aslant like an enormous octopus at yoga.

We wait for a big
break in the traffic
and cross.
At the tree Dragon provides the foothold,
pushes us up
with all her strength
into the lowest branch, where we sit for a second
to get our breath,
then pull ourselves up higher
into the second storey of branches.

The traffic drowns out the sounds
of night creatures.

The lights from the city suppress the stars.

'Doesn't matter what happens tomorrow.
We've gone further
than anyone ever expected,'
Tippi says,
letting her leg dangle over the grassy knoll below.
And I know she is not talking about climbing

this tree.
'I'm almost happy.
Aren't you?'

A tractor trundles by on the access road.

The air is cold.

'I'm happy,' I say.
'But I'm so scared.
What if I wake up and you've gone?
I don't want to wake up without you.'

A team of fire trucks whirr and their
red lights flicker.
As they speed by
        the traffic slows and
        parts to let them go—
        this desperate cavalry.

'Are you coming down?' Dragon shouts.

'Are we?' I ask Tippi.

'Of course we're going down,' she says.
'We're going down together.'

Nil by Mouth

Tippi asks a nurse for water but is refused—
'It might interfere with what the anaesthetists have
   planned,'
the nurse explains.
'But let me go and get you some ice chips.'

Tippi throws up her hands.
'I cannot believe we haven't been offered a last meal,'
she says,
even though we stuffed ourselves
silly on cake and cookies
all afternoon.

Grammie pinches Tippi's ear.
'Last meals are for suckers on death row.
And you are going to be *fine*.'

Tippi doesn't quote statistics
but pinches her back and says,
'If I were your age, I'd be having my last meal
   every night.'

Dad guffaws and prods Grammie playfully.
She sticks out her tongue.
'I'll outlive you all,' she says.

At once the room goes quiet.

It is the last thing Grammie says before
she leaves in tears.

Humankind Cannot Bear Very Much Reality

'I'm not going to come to the hospital in the
  morning,'
Dragon says before she leaves.
She leans back into her heels,
sucks at her bottom lip.
'I think I'll spend the day at the studio.
I've a show in a week and my turns are sloppy.
I hope you don't mind.
I hope you don't think—'

'Of course not, Dragon,' we say together.
We understand she wants to be distracted.
And we don't need her spending twenty-four hours
gazing into a vending machine
and waiting for the operating room doors to open,
for Dr Derrick to appear with the report
written in his eyes.

'But I'll be thinking about you.
I want you to know—'
She pauses, hugs herself, and looks at each of us.

Tippi then me.

Tippi then me.

'I want you to know—'
she tries again,
but she cannot finish.
Her voice splinters
and the tears come.

'I know what you want to say,' I manage.
'It's OK not to say it.'

She kisses us each on the cheek
then gasping for breath
turns quickly
and runs from the room.

Code Red

The night nurse,
a barrelling woman in her fifties with
tight grey curls
and a faint moustache,
comes into our room
      with a tiny bottle of what looks like
      red nail polish.
'I've been told to paint Grace's fingernails,'
she says.
'The doctors want to know
which heart has the problem.'
She attempts to smile
but it gets lost before her lips
can curl all the way
upwards.

'I'll paint them,' Tippi says,
and takes the polish from the nurse
who won't leave until every nail
is red.

'Thank you,' I tell Tippi,
who is blowing on my fingernails
as she always does,

and
I tell myself
that this makes perfect sense—
that the doctors *should* be playing it safe
to prevent any mistakes tomorrow.
But I can't help thinking that
the red polish is telling the doctors
less about whose heart to look out for
and more about
the life they should relinquish
if it comes to it.

Before Bed

I unlatch the rabbit's foot pendant from
around my neck
and put it on the nightstand
before turning out the light.

I don't want it any more.

I don't need it.

Luck is a lie.

All Night

All night Tippi and I lie with our arms
wrapped around each other
like rope.
I bury my face in her neck
and she wakes every now and then
to kiss the top of my head.
When the birds begin to sing
and the sky turns peachy,
we lie looking at each other,
our eyes too tired for tears.
Tippi rubs my nose with her own.
'It's all going to be OK,' she says.
'And even if it's not OK. It really is.'

JANUARY 21ST

Separation Day

Mom is clutching our hands and Dad is holding her
  up.
'We love you,
we love you,
we love you,' they say
over and over
like an incantation.
A nurse drags them away
and the swing doors to the operating room gobble
  us up.

It seems like a thousand people are in the room
and when we enter they are silent.

Dr Derrick takes centre stage.
        'Ready?' he asks.

We are nudged on to the operating table
like meat on to a chopping block.

'As ready as we ever will be,' Tippi says.

Dr Derrick leans down so only we can hear him.
'I'll do my best
to keep you together.
I'll do my very, very best,' he whispers.

I squeeze Tippi's hand and she rolls her head to the
  side
to look at me squarely.
'See you soon, sister,' she says
and presses her lips against mine
like she did when we were little.

'Soon,' I say.

We rest our heads against each other
and suck in silence.

JANUARY 29TH

I Move My Head to Look for Tippi

She is not here.
Not beside me in the bed
nor in the room
at all.

It has happened.

I am alive and I am
alone
in a land of
so much
space.

It has happened.

Sick

Mom, Dad, and Grammie are squeezing different
parts of my body,
gripping on to me like I might
float away if they didn't.
Dragon stands at the end of the bed.
Her eyes are red-rimmed,
her face wrung out.
Mom sobs.
Dad sniffs.
Grammie's nostrils quiver.
Dragon is the only person who can talk.
'Your body is doing well with the Heartware,' she
tells me.
'And they've put you on a list.
You're on a list to get a heart, Grace.'
A twisted smile.
'But Tippi is not doing so well.
She lost a lot of blood during the operation
and now
she has an infection.
She's pretty sick.
Like,
she's very sick.'

'I want to see her,' I say.
'I want to be with her.'

Dragon nods.
'We knew you'd say that.'

Holding On

Tippi is hooked up to as many wires and tubes as I
am.
She is lying in a quarantined room,
doctors darkly mumbling and skulking in a
corner,
a monitor persistently beeping
next to her.

The huge wound at my hip burns.
My stomach clenches.
Swallowing slices my throat.

'Put me next to her,' I say.

The doctors shake their heads and
the nurses bow because there's no way they will
defy their superiors.

'Let me lie next to her,' I beg.

Dad grunts and without asking permission,
pushes my trolley bed as close to Tippi's as he can.
'Help me move your sister,' he tells Dragon,
and suddenly the doctors dart across the room

and
I slide gently
on to Tippi's bed
along with a bag
the size of a laptop
that is keeping me alive.

My body pounds and I scream out.

But still Tippi does not move.

Her breath is as delicate as lace,
her face is calm
like she never expected this to go any other way.

I put my arms around her.

Hold on.

Sinking

In the morning Tippi's eyes are
narrow slits letting in hardly any light.
I use my fingertips to stroke her lips.
'Hello,' she says
in a barely-there voice
and again, 'Hello.'

Against the pain, I press my chest into her,
try to make our bodies merge.

She winces and shakes her head.
'I'm sinking,' she says.

'You're not,' I lie.

Tippi manages a little laugh,
all her skepticism wrapped up in it.
'Remember your promise,' she tells me.

What am I supposed to do?
I don't know
so I say the words I would want to hear,
'Go, if you have to.'

A corner of Tippi's mouth lifts as
her eyes close.

Her eyes close
and they do not open.

'Go,' I repeat.
'Go, go, go.'

Gone

Dr Derrick stands over me in a clean white coat,
his stethoscope dangling
like an ugly necklace.

Dad is next to him,
a greying beard grown in.
Mom is by the door
in shadow.

'Can you hear me?' Dr Derrick asks.

I can hear but
I do not move.

I blink and he speaks.

'Tippi's gone,' he says.
'All I can say is I'm sorry.
I'm so, so sorry,
but I know that's not enough.'

'Get out,' I say,
turning away from everyone and
hating them all equally.

Tippi

Tippi? Tippi? Tippi? Tippi? Tippi? Tippi? Tippi?
Tippi? Tippi? Tippi? Tippi? Tippi? Tippi? Tippi?
Tippi? Tippi? Tippi? Tippi? Tippi? Tippi? Tippi?
Tippi? Tippi? Tippi? Tippi? Tippi? Tippi? Tippi?
Tippi? Tippi? Tippi? Tippi? Tippi? Tippi? Tippi?
Tippi? Tippi? Tippi? Tippi? Tippi? Tippi? Tippi?
Tippi? Tippi? Tippi? Tippi? Tippi? Tippi? Tippi?
Tippi? Tippi? Tippi? Tippi? Tippi? Tippi? Tippi?
Tippi? Tippi? Tippi? Tippi? Tippi? Tippi? Tippi?
Tippi? Tippi? Tippi? Tippi? Tippi? Tippi? Tippi?
Tippi.

I Ache

I howl and I scream.
I ache for my sister.
'Tippi,' I whisper into the darkness.

I howl and I scream.
I ache for my sister.
'Tippi!' I beg from the darkness.

I howl and I scream.
I ache for my sister.
I howl and I scream.
I ache for my sister.

I ache for my sister in my blood and bones
in my limbs and my veins.
I ache for myself.
'I love you,' I tell her
and I ache.

'I miss you,' I tell her
and I ache.

And this aching,
this aching,
it will not
go away.

Her Heart

I want it in me.
I do not want them to throw it away.
I want it in me.
To save me.
To save it.
To save her.
A little bit of her.

'Tippi's heart wasn't healthy enough
to use in any transplant,' Dr Derrick's
voice mutters.
'And anyway, it's too late.
It's far too late for that
now.'

And I know it's true.
But it is such a waste.
Tippi always had
a very strong
heart.

Healing

A nurse with wire-brush hair is by my side.
A latex glove presses on my arm.

My body burns from the
inside
out.
I feel banging in my bones,
thudding behind my ribs,
a stabbing like glass is being injected
all over my skin.

The pain is exhausting and endless.

It is
more than I ever imagined
I could feel.

I croak
and the latex tightens around my arm.
'Are you hurting?' the nurse asks.

'Yes,' I tell her.

She fiddles with a bag of clear solution
hanging by my bed
as though a morphine refill will fix me.

'All better soon,' she says.

But how can that be true?
How can anything she gives me
take away this pain?

Voices by My Bed

She needs
some fresh air.
She needs
more meds.
She needs
to get home.
She needs
our prayers.
She needs
her family here,
her friends close by.
She needs
a chance to grieve,
a chance to talk,
a chance to laugh.
She needs
water,
drugs,
silence,
time.

But I need
none
of these things.

What I need
is
Tippi.

FEBRUARY

Improvement

Today I have eaten half a cracker,
and the doctors are pleased.

Anorexic

Dragon is the first person I agree to see.
She sits on my right,
not trying to fill the void on my left,
and talks about the weather—
the snow which is three feet high
in Hoboken today.
And about Dad who has
moved back home
and hasn't had a drink
for weeks, as far as she can tell.

Dragon's bones poke through her skin.
Her gaunt face is ghostly.
'Are you anorexic?' I ask,
suddenly sure she is and angry with myself
for not saying something sooner.

She nods. 'Probably.'

'That would have pissed Tippi off,' I tell her.
'We'll have to do something about it.'

Dragon puts her head on my pillow
and squeaks out a cry.
'I miss her, too,' she says.
'We all do.
So, so much.'

Recovery

I tell Mom not to postpone the funeral,
that I'll be in the hospital many months
and I don't want to make Tippi wait.

Instead I get Paul to record the service
—which he does—
then he leaves a slim silver DVD next to my bedside
so I can see how it happened.

When I am stronger, I will watch.

I will watch my
Aunty Anne singing about a bird with wide wings,
Yasmeen reading a poem about
carrying the dead's heart in our hearts,
my father, uncles, and Jon carrying Tippi's coffin
to a hole in the earth and
lowering her into it.

I will do all of this.
But for now I am in the hospital recovering,
letting the wounds heal
and waiting for the doctors to cut out my heart
and replace it with one that's not broken.

'Time is a healer,' Dr Murphy tells me,
and though I don't believe her,
I let time pass.

I let time pass
and
I live.

I live in hope
that soon,
very soon,
another human heart
will be stuffed
inside me.
I live in hope
that a dead person's heart will
revive me.

MARCH

Speaking

Caroline comes alone,
no Paul or Shane,
just her and a camera,
though she says it's too soon.

Maybe she's right but she
sets up at
the end of my bed and
starts rolling
anyway.

'I want to talk,' I say.
'I want to speak it out.'

'Fine,' Caroline says.

I turn my head to the left
to let Tippi start,
forgetting that I am a singleton.

This will happen
for the rest of my life:
I will never remember that she has gone.

'Go on,' Caroline says.

And I do.

I go on.

My Story

This is my story.
It is mine alone because I am the one who needs
to tell it.
I am the one who is still here,
no longer stage right but

centre stage.

It is a single story,
not two tales tangled up in each other
like lovers' limbs,
as you might expect.

And anyway, Tippi was
always pretty good at getting heard.

I have hidden from the world for a long time.

I have been a coward.

But here is my story.

The story of how it is to be Two.
The story of how it is to be One.

The Story of Us.

And it is an epitaph.

An epitaph to love.

Author's Note

Although this novel is a work of fiction, the lives of Tippi and Grace, their feelings about being conjoined, and many of the details about how the public treats them, are based on amalgamated stories of real-life conjoined twins, both living and dead. Particularly helpful books have been *Conjoined Twins: An Historical, Biological and Ethical Issues Encyclopedia*, by Christine Quigley, and *Very Special People*, by Frederick Drimmer, as well as a score of documentaries on the subject, most notably BBC2's 'Horizon: Conjoined Twins' and BBC3's 'Abby and Brittany: Joined for Life'.

The ethicist Alice Dreger's writings on conjoined twins and people living with unusual anatomies have also profoundly informed my views on separation surgery. As all cases of conjoined twins are unique, the hypothetical medical situations in this novel are based on conversations with leading heart specialists from University College London, Great Ormond Street Hospital for Children, and particularly with Edward Kiely, one of the world's leading surgeons for conjoined twins.

It might be astounding to a singleton, but conjoined twins do not see themselves or their lives as tragedies. Two such twins are Abby and Brittany Hensel, born in Minnesota in 1990, who have said they never wish to be parted. Abby and Brittany have appeared on many TV shows and in documentaries in the hope that by allowing the public into their lives, they will be left to live as normally as possible. They have completed college, travelled to Europe with their friends, and now work as elementary school teachers. They are a testament to the fact that separation, especially a separation which puts one particular twin at great risk, isn't always the best option.

Many conjoined twins have lived full and happy lives, and several have married and had children. Arguably the most famous conjoined twins in history were Chang and Eng Bunker (originally from what was then called Siam, hence the term 'Siamese twins') whom I reference in this novel. They married a pair of American sisters, shared their time between two homes, and fathered twenty-one children. Their descendants continue to meet regularly and celebrate the legacy of these two men.

That isn't to say that all conjoined twins have had it easy. The physiology of Tippi and Grace is loosely based on the bodies of Masha and Dasha Krivoshlyapova, whose mother was told they had died at birth and who were then experimented on for over twenty years by Russian scientists. Most conjoined twins are stillborn and those that do survive have short lives due to their physical abnormalities—often congenital heart defects.

Researching this novel has been painful. I have spent many hours in tears as I read or watched stories about parents losing their children or one twin losing his or her sibling. But ultimately, writing this novel has been a huge honour. It has been invaluable to me, not just as a writer, but as a parent, friend, wife and daughter, to have been given the time and space to think about what it means to be an individual and more importantly, what it really means to love another person.

Acknowledgements

Some people deserve to be mentioned. Loads more than I have space for here. But special thanks to my agent Julia Churchill for being supportive of this project from the very beginning. Thank you to my sensitive and careful editors Martha Mihalick and Zöe Griffiths and to everyone in the teams at Greenwillow, New York, and Bloomsbury, London, for being so darn brilliant—always.

Also have it known that I am indebted to the following for various acts of support, generosity, kindness, hard work, or bravery: Professor Aroon Hingorani, Professor Andrew Taylor, Mr Edward Kiely, The British Library, Repforce Ireland, Combined Media, Jennifer Custer, Hélène Ferey, Chris Slegg, Emma Bradshaw, Zareena Huber, Nikki Sheehan and Ani Luca. Thanks, of course, to my friends and family, especially Andreas, Aoife, Jimmy, Mum, Dad, and the Donegal and New Jersey clans, for their ongoing love—you rock the party!

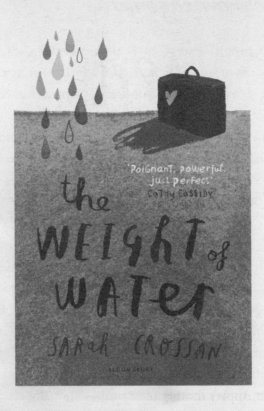

'Poignant, powerful,
just perfect'
Cathy Cassidy

the
WEIGHT of
WATER

SARAH CROSSAN

BLOOMSBURY

Armed with a suitcase and an old laundry bag,
Kasienka and her mother head for England.
Life is lonely for Kasienka. At home her mother's
heart is breaking; at school friends are scarce.
But when someone special swims into her life,
Kasienka learns that there might be more
than one way for her to stay afloat.

'A poignant, realistic tale about learning to love' SUNDAY TIMES

APPLE AND RAIN

SHORTLISTED
CILIP
Carnegie Medal
2015

SARAH CROSSAN

BLOOMSBURY

When Apple's mother returns after eleven years away,
Apple feels whole again. She will have an answer
to her burning question – why did you go?
But just like the stormy Christmas Eve when she left,
her mother's homecoming is bitter sweet.
It's only when Apple meets someone more lost
than she is, that she begins to see things
as they really are.